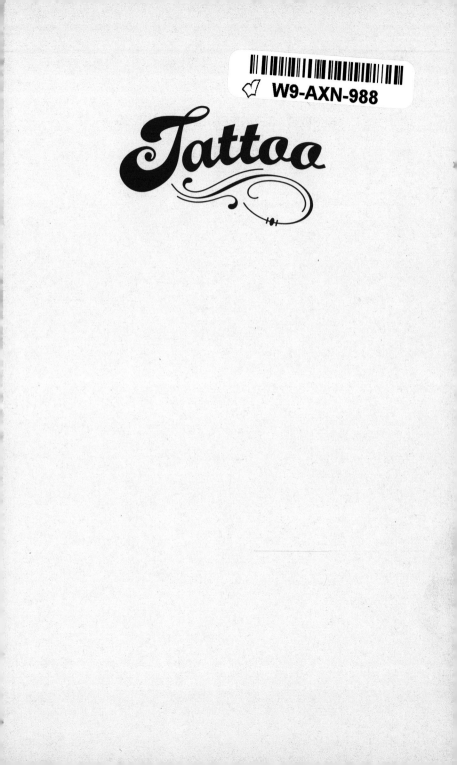

Tattoo

JENNIFER LYNN BARNES

Tattoo

DELACORTE PRESS

Published by Delacorte Press
an imprint of Random House Children's Books
a division of Random House, Inc.
New York

www.randomhouse.com/teens

Educators and librarians, for a variety of teaching tools, visit us at
www.randomhouse.com/teachers

Library of Congress Cataloging-in-Publication Data
Barnes, Jennifer (Jennifer Lynn)
Tattoo / by Jennifer Lynn Barnes. —1st ed.
p. cm.
Summary: When four fifteen-year-old friends share the temporary tattoos
they bought from a mysterious woman at the mall, each develops psychic
powers that will help them fight the ancient being who plans to wreak
havoc at their school dance.
ISBN 978-0-385-73347-2 (tr. pbk.)—ISBN 978-0-385-90363-9 (glb)
[1. Psychic ability—Fiction. 2. Supernatural—Fiction. 3. Best Friends—
Fiction. 4. Friendship—Fiction. 5. Mythology—Fiction. 6. Humorous
stories.] I. Title.
PZ7.B26225Tat 2006
[Fic]—dc22   2005035799

The text of this book is set in 11-point Galliard.

Book design by Trish Parcell Watts

Printed in the United States of America

10 9 8 7 6 5

First Edition

To the ladies of the Naked Left Pinkie Toe—
you know who you are

Chapter 1

"Passion Purple, Fruity Fuchsia, Playful Pink." Delia Cameron smiled as she came to the rose-colored nail polish. According to Delia, pink was the new pink. She'd tried to explain it to me once in terms of the color orange, but fashion wasn't really my forte, and I was pretty sure I had completely missed the point. At the age of fifteen, I more or less had to face the fact that, unlike my best friend—Delia Cameron, fashion goddess—there was a distinct chance that I didn't actually *have* a forte.

"Divine Yellow," Delia continued, picking up the next nail polish container on the shelf and examining it like a detective looking for clues in a case of paramount importance.

Beside me, Annabelle grinned wryly, and the half

smile softened her typically solemn features. To the outside world, Annabelle Porter was an almost alien creature: quiet and shy, too serious for her own good, and too smart for anyone else's. Once upon a time (in the seventh grade), she'd seemed that way to me, too, but now—three years, two hundred and six sleepovers, thirteen embarrassing karaoke nights I'm sure we'd all rather forget, and an unofficial initiation into our tight little group later, I knew Annabelle well enough to know that the crooked half smile was some kind of commentary on Delia's nail polish manifesto.

I grinned at Annabelle, and she bit back a bigger smile. We'd both been in this exact position many, many times before.

Blissfully unaware (or maybe deliberately ignoring) the silent exchange between the two of us, Delia picked up another bottle of polish and became instantly and absolutely entranced by it. "Mango Mermaid," she breathed in the reverent tone most people reserved for the birth of their first child.

"Mango Mermaid?" the fourth member of our group asked, her voice low, dry, and incredulous. She looked at me. "Mango Mermaid," she repeated flatly, shooting me a tortured look.

I patted her consolingly on the shoulder. Poor Zo. Shopping with Delia took a certain kind of endurance, and Zo Porter, Annabelle's cousin and more or less my other half for practically as long as either of us could remember, didn't have it.

"Yes," Delia replied, rolling her eyes at Zo. "Mango Mermaid. Just look at the shimmer and composition. It's perfect."

"We've found the perfect nail polish," Zo said, her voice still completely flat. "Hurrah." With a tiny, almost pixie-like build, blond hair, and baby blue eyes, Zo didn't exactly look like your typical tomboy, but there was no mistaking the fact that she was anti-girly and had been even before the day her mother had dropped five-year-old Zo off at my house for playgroup, left the state, and never looked back.

Delia, the Mango Mermaid polish held safely in her left hand, tucked a strand of chestnut brown hair behind her ear with her right. In typical Delia fashion, she was completely unaffected by Zo's scorn for all things feminine. "Says the girl wearing her brother's sweatshirt," Delia said, eyeing Zo's gray sweats disapprovingly.

"I don't have a brother," Zo said immediately.

Delia arched one eyebrow. "Oh," she said with a look of faux surprise. "My mistake."

Annabelle watched the repartee between her cousin and Delia and then tilted her head to the side. "Did you hear that?" she asked me.

"What?" I asked. I saw the twinkle in her eye a moment too late.

"That," she said, her voice as soft and serious as always, "was the sound of civility flying out the window."

Zo, Delia, and I had been best friends for as long as any of us could remember. The two of them liked to pretend that they just tolerated each other for my sake, but in reality, arguing was practically an Olympic sport with those two, and there was no one Delia would rather argue with than Zo. I, for one, wasn't fooled by their little act, and civility comments aside, neither was Annabelle.

"Food court?" I suggested out loud, knowing that there were exactly two reasons Zo put up with our Friday afternoon mall trips. The first was because the rest of us liked the mall, and tough-girl act aside, there wasn't anything short of breast implants that Zo wouldn't have done for the rest of us. The second, more compelling reason Zo tolerated our weekly mall trips was the triple chili-cheese dog, bacon cheeseburger, and chocolate milkshake she ate every time we went to the food court.

"It's about time," Zo said, making a big show of grumbling. Still, she picked up a second Mango Mermaid polish and tossed it underhand to Delia. "I'm starving," she said by way of explanation, "and these are buy-one-get-one-free."

Wisely, Annabelle, Delia, and I said nothing about the fact that Zo had eaten right before we left. Her endless appetite and teeny tiny body size were almost as much of a mystery to me as Delia's innate understanding of all things fashion and the fact that Annabelle could say more with a single look than I could with an entire sentence.

With a toss of her hair, Delia flounced off to buy the

Mango Mermaid polish, and five minutes later, the four of us stepped out of the store and into the the open expanse of the mall.

"You know what I love about the mall?" Delia asked, her voice bright.

"The sales?" I asked.

"Your father's credit card?" Annabelle asked with another Annabelle half grin.

"The torture?" Zo hadn't quite given up playing the shopping martyr.

"No, no, and don't kid yourself," Delia said, responding to us in order. "The smell."

I sniffed the air cautiously while Zo and Annabelle, for once in their lives on the same page, shared a look of confusion.

"I don't smell anything," I said. I paused for a moment, wondering if I should even go there. "What does it smell like?" I swiftly maneuvered around a cart selling neon cell-phone accessories as I spoke. Unfortunately, I was maneuvering a little *too* swiftly and ended up running face-first into the next cart. For a split second, I fought to keep my balance. I lost, and crashed to the floor with the grace of an overweight elephant.

"Now that ain't pretty," Zo said before dispensing what passed in her mind as helpful advice. "Lift foot, then shift weight, Bay."

"I didn't trip," I replied, narrowing my eyes at her. "I ran into—"

"Possibilities," Delia interjected happily.

5

"Huh?" She'd lost me with that comment.

"I smell possibilities," Delia said, stepping over me to get to the booth. "The mall is filled with possibilities. Take these earrings, for example."

Zo groaned loudly. "Hungry," she reminded us.

Delia waved the complaint aside with a delicate flick of her right hand.

Not wanting to get caught in the middle of their weekly mall showdown, I started to stand up, and as I did, I felt a hand on my arm, pulling me to my feet.

"Thanks," I said, dusting myself off and turning around. "I . . ."

As soon as I saw his eyes, my mouth stopped functioning, which was a good thing, because my brain had clicked off a microsecond before.

Kane Lawson, eye candy. King of eye candy. God of eye candy.

"Thanks," I said, forcing myself to form a decipherable word while my mind froze from cuteness overload. Emergency, emergency, I thought. Must form coherent sentence.

"What are you boys doing here?" Delia asked, never at a loss for words, especially around members of the opposite sex.

Boys as in plural? I wondered at her words and looked past Kane to see two of his friends. It was like eye candy, supersized.

"Just hanging out," Kane said, his hand still on mine. "You okay?"

No, I wanted to reply. Put me in ICU, fatal embarrassment ward.

"I'm . . ." I searched for the right word, my brain being difficult.

"Fine?" Zo prodded.

"That," I said weakly. For good measure, I nodded vigorously, as if that was somehow going to make me appear like less of a total and complete idiot.

Unlike Delia, who had a new crush every week, I'd had exactly two in my entire lifetime. The first had been a deep and undying love for the boy with curly brown hair in my kindergarten class. The second was Kane.

"You're Hayley, right?" Kane asked me, filling the silence. "I think you're in my geometry class."

"Bailey," I corrected him, my name getting caught in my throat. "And it's world history."

He nodded and smiled. Oh, the smile.

Delia began chatting up the guy on the left while the guy to Kane's right raked his eyes up and down, first over Annabelle's body and then over Zo's. Apparently, even in her sweats, she was more appealing than I was. Story of my life.

"Hey, buddy," Zo said, her voice casual yet deadly. "Eyes on face."

Annabelle stifled a laugh, and I groaned inwardly. Zo had no tact and even less impulse control, and despite the fact that she wasn't an inch over five feet tall, the look she was giving the guy to my right had me convinced that if he didn't manage to drag his eyes away from the perfect figure hidden under her sweat suit, he'd find himself in a world of pain within the next thirty seconds.

"Bailey," Kane said again, repeating my name and drawing my attention away from Zo. I looked over at him, and for a moment, we just stared at each other. Finally, he nodded at me and smiled. "See you around."

I nodded dumbly, a smile plastered on my face. Kane Lawson would see me around.

The guys took off, and the moment they were out of earshot, Delia squealed. "What did he say?" she asked.

"See you around," I said. He'd now officially said over a hundred words to me. It had taken five years to get there, but I was finally in the triple digits.

Delia pondered my words. "Was it 'I'll see you around' or 'see you around' or 'see ya around'?" she asked seriously.

"That matters?" I asked.

Delia nodded. "When it comes to guys," she said, "everything matters."

"Everything matters," a musical voice repeated. I turned and found myself staring into eyes so blue it almost hurt to look at them. "Can I help you girls with anything?" the woman asked, gesturing toward the booth.

Zo glanced at Delia and then back at the saleswoman. "Don't encourage her," she said flatly.

I looked at the woman, unable to turn my gaze from

her eyes, all thoughts of Kane exiting my mind as I stared into them.

"I need something cutting-edge that will flatter a retrochic red-carpet look," Delia said.

Zo fought a smile and shrugged at the saleswoman. "I told you not to encourage her."

The woman clicked her tongue and murmured quietly as she pulled open a drawer on top of the booth. "Try this," she suggested, handing Delia a black metal choker with a small white bow in the middle. "It's retro and cutting."

She turned her attention to Zo. "And for you," she said.

Zo held up one hand in protest. "Oh no," she said. "I'm not interested. I don't do accessories."

The woman ignored her and held out a small, deep purple crystal on an almost invisible gold chain. It swung back and forth in front of Zo's face, and despite herself, Zo was captivated.

Watching the crystal, I felt my mind drifting off, and I could practically hear the woman going all "you're getting sleepy, verrrrryyyy sleepy" on me. I shook my head to clear my thoughts.

"And for you," the saleswoman continued, turning to Annabelle as she placed the crystal firmly in Zo's callused hand. "You're not going to argue with me like this one?" she asked, nodding her head toward Zo.

"Zo and I are very different," Annabelle, queen of the understatement, said evenly.

Zo snorted under her breath. She was the only person who could actually get a rise out of A-belle. Since they were first cousins and only children, I'd always thought it was a sibling rivalry kind of thing.

"For you, something classic," the woman said to Annabelle. "Understated."

"Practical," Annabelle put in, and Zo snorted again. Annabelle was one of those rare people who was born practical. Of course, the fact that she'd grown up all over the world with a linguist mother and an anthropologist father surrounded only by adults might have had something to do with it, too.

The woman measured Annabelle's request. "Sometimes," she murmured. "Sometimes practical. Observant certainly, and true."

Why did I feel as if I'd called one of those psychic hotlines? 1-800-CREEPYSALESLADY.

The woman's blue eyes flittered over to me as she ran her fingers along the edges of several silver barrettes. I looked at her face, and my teeth ached with the sheer blueness of those eyes.

"This," the woman said, closing her hands over a circular dark silver barrette and turning back to Annabelle. "This is for you."

I looked at my friend. In true Annabelle style, she didn't say anything. Instead, she flipped the barrette over in her hand to look at the price, and after a moment, she nodded.

"Okay," she said simply. Her mouth curved into a slow grin. "I like it."

I bit my bottom lip and waited. The woman said nothing.

"What about Bailey?" Delia asked, still admiring her necklace. "She could benefit from a little accessorizing. Trust me." Delia didn't mean anything by it, and since she'd been saying pretty much the exact same thing since we were four years old, I didn't take offense. In the world of Delia Cameron, shopping goddess, everyone needed fashion advice, except, of course, for Delia.

"For you," the woman said. For a second, I heard nothing but that melodic voice. The rest of the sounds of the mall faded away, and the colors in front of my eyes swirled and blended together in the background until all I could see was the woman. "It is not I who can choose for you."

Her words echoed in my head.

"You must choose for yourself."

There was no way to argue with the command. When I thought about it, it was kind of pathetic that I couldn't even argue with the kiosk lady. Chalk another one up for Bailey Morgan, high school doormat.

With great effort, I pulled my attention away from the woman's eyes and my own thoughts and turned to look at the booth. Jewelry of all kinds hung on dainty displays. Cautiously, I let my finger trail over a watch with a face like the view of a river from a plane, carved into wood.

The woman watched me carefully, but I shook my head. As I pulled my hand back from the watch, my shirt caught on a small drawer and pulled it open. Startled, I backed up, unaware that my sleeve had attached itself to the drawer. Its contents poured out onto the floor, clattering loudly enough that everyone within a fifty-foot radius turned to look at me in one coordinated motion.

Maybe being a klutz was my forte.

"I am so sorry," I said. Even to my ears, my voice sounded high-pitched. I just don't deal well with pressure.

I bent down to pick up the rings and stones that had fallen out of the drawer, and something caught my eye. A piece of paper? Somehow, it didn't quite fit with the rest of the jewelry. I picked it up and discovered that it was covered in protective plastic. I turned it over, and as I did, words flashed in front of my eyes, filling the top of the page.

" 'Temporary tattoos,' " I read out loud.

"Oh, coolies," Delia said. "You should totally go for it, Bay."

I brought my finger to touch the plastic over the tattoos. There were four of them, all a deep blue-green.

Sidhe blue. Blood green.

The words echoed in my head as I traced my fingers along the lines of one of the tattoos. They didn't form any recognizable shape that I could see, twisting and turning and melting into one another in odd forms that burned themselves into my mind.

"I'd rather have the real thing," Zo said. She'd been talking about getting a tattoo since she was nine.

"Really, Zo?" Annabelle asked in one of those two-word sentences that actually conveyed a five-minute speech about how much Zo's dad would freak out.

Zo shrugged. "It might be worth it," she said, casting an impish grin in my direction.

"Or," I said, eyeing the tattoos, "it might not."

"Well, are you getting them or aren't you?" Delia asked impatiently. "Thoughtful shopping is a plus, but indecisive shopping? Major weakness, Bailey."

I nodded, trying to digest the fact that Delia had just accused me of being a weak shopper. "Okay," I said. "I'll take them."

The saleswoman's blue eyes stared through me and into me at the same time, sharp and searching. "Are you sure?"

Delia took the tattoos from me and placed them on the counter in front of the cash register. "She's sure," she said, making the decision for me.

One by one, we paid for our purchases, and by the time we were done, Delia was practically dancing with shopping-fueled euphoria. "How lucky was that? I mean, accessories can make or break an outfit, and to find so many . . ." She trailed off. "And you'll share the tattoos, yes, Bailey?" she asked, half command, half question.

I looked down at the plain silver bag in which I carried my sole purchase for the day. "Yeah," I said. "Of course."

"So hot," Delia said. "This is going to be so hot. Dibs on the swirly one."

"They're Bailey's," Zo said immediately. She'd been watching out for me for so long that by now, it was more or less automatic. "Shouldn't she get dibs?" Zo put air quotes around the word "dibs." Clearly, it wasn't a normal part of her vocabulary.

Delia narrowed her eyes at Zo, and I could sense another softly sarcastic comment coming from Annabelle's general direction, but a second later, Delia shrugged. "Sureness," she said, slinging an arm around my shoulder. "Whatever you want, Bay."

I glanced at Zo and bit back a smile. "Food," I said, speaking for both of us. "I want food."

And with that, we headed for the food court as Delia began an extensive discourse on our outfit options for the upcoming dance. Zo walked on my other side, hands in her pockets, and Annabelle followed a step behind us.

Just another Friday afternoon at the mall.

We totally should have known better.

Chapter 2

"Yes, yes, no, and *what* were you thinking?" Delia passed judgment on our outfits one by one as we came out of our dressing rooms to stand in front of the three-way mirror. She and I had gotten yeses, and Annabelle had been the no. Zo looked down at the sport pants and T-shirt she'd found in the faux-exercise section of Escape, Delia's favorite store and our current location.

"What's wrong with this?" Zo asked defensively. Annabelle looked down at her own floor-length skirt with a frown.

"We're talking about a dance here, Zo, not dance class."

As if Zo had ever in her life stepped inside a ballet studio.

With a thoughtful expression on her face, Delia

stalked away and came back a few minutes later with a tiny black dress. She held it out to Zo and pointed firmly to the dressing room.

Zo snorted. "Queenie, you gotta be out of your mind." From Zo, "Queenie" was a term of endearment. Sort of.

Delia just kept pointing. Beside me, Annabelle was trying very hard not to smile. The rest of the week, no one told Zo Porter what to do, but the mall was Delia's turf, not Zo's, and with a glower that was more for show than anything else, Zo disappeared back into the dressing room.

Annabelle waited patiently, preparing herself for Hurricane Delia, the fashion tornado.

"You need to show a little more skin," Delia said. She looked the outfit up and down. "The colors aren't bad, and it fits well, but . . ."

"No." Annabelle just shook her head. "I like it."

"Oh." Delia paused. Zo she could argue with, but on the rare occasions that Annabelle actually verbally expressed an opinion, nothing and no one could change her mind.

"You did say it was a good color and fit well," I told Delia consolingly. Then I turned to Annabelle. "And don't feel bad that your outfit didn't make the Delia cut," I told her. "The only reason mine did is because Delia picked it out to begin with."

"There is that," Delia admitted with a good-natured

smile, bouncing back from the minor fashion defeat. "Zo, what's taking so long?"

"Do you know how many straps this thing has?" Zo sounded so incredulous and puzzled that as her voice floated over the dressing room door, I giggled.

"While we're waiting . . ." Delia popped into my open dressing room and back out a moment later with a giant smile on her face. "Tattoos!"

She wiggled the sheet at us, her eyes lighting up with the motion.

"I thought you wanted to save those for the dance," I said.

Delia scanned the back of the package. "No instructions," she said. "It just says three days." She paused for a moment. "Friday to Saturday, Saturday to Sunday, Sunday to Monday. Perfect."

Her words echoed in my head.

Three days.

Perfect.

"Though the fact that our school is having the biggest dance of the year on a Monday night," she continued, "is just plain wrong. Evil, really."

"You wanna see evil?" Zo asked from inside the dressing room, where I could only assume she was still recovering from waging a losing battle with the straps. "Look in the mirror."

"You have the dress on, don't you?" Delia asked with a huge smile.

Silence.

"I think she dooooeeees," I said, dragging out the word.

"Come on, Zo," Annabelle prodded, picking up my teasing tone and making it her own. "Let us see." She paused and winked at me. "I bet it looks *pretty*."

Annabelle knew exactly how to press Zo's buttons.

"Shut it, A-belle," Zo growled.

Annabelle shrugged and shut her mouth, an evil, almost little-sister-like grin on her face.

"While we're waiting," Delia said, emphasizing the word "waiting," "you want to do the honors, Bay?" She held the package of tattoos out to me.

For a moment, I stared at them through some kind of haze, feeling my blood pump through my veins and listening to the rush of it in my ears.

"Bailey?" Annabelle asked, gently touching my shoulder. "Are you okay?"

"I'm fine." I forced myself to focus and took the tattoos from Delia's outstretched hands to "do the honors" and open them. The moment my hand touched the package, a chill ran from the base of my neck down my spine. I stared at the four tattoos and ran my finger over the top of the package. Gingerly, I tugged at the plastic cover, but it didn't move. I tightened my grip and tried again. The second I felt the packaging give under the pressure, I closed my eyes.

To fight, to live
We two of three bestow this gift. . . .

"Bailey? Earth to Bailey, do you read us?"

"Now that," I said under my breath, "was freaky."

"What?" all three of my friends asked at once, Zo's voice muffled from behind the dressing room door.

"Voices," I replied. "In my head. They were saying something about gift bestowing. . . ." About that time, I realized that I sounded completely insane, and I decided that it wasn't the world's best idea for me to go around talking about the voices in my head, especially in public places. "Just kidding," I amended. "What are you guys, the gullibility triplets?"

Annabelle looked at me, her face carefully blank and her eyes measuring. After a long pause, she reached into her purse and pulled out a pair of scissors.

When the Boy Scouts said "be prepared," they'd never met Annabelle. She brought new definition to the word.

Delia daintily plucked the tattoos out of my hand and took the scissors from A-belle. With one clean snip, she had a tattoo in her hand. "It kind of looks like a butterfly . . . or half of a butterfly," Delia said. "Except for this line here." She ran her finger down the center of the symbol.

Annabelle took the tattoos and touched the edge of one of them. Where Delia's had been two gently intersecting circles divided by a single curving line, the tattoo Annabelle was pointing to was thinner and longer, like two crescent moons crossing paths. Or, I realized, like two freakishly shaped eyeballs staring at me.

"Take it," I said, answering the question in her eyes with a shudder. "It's yours."

Annabelle took the scissors from Delia and made quick work of cutting out the tattoo. With mock solemnity, she handed the rest of the sheet to me.

I looked down at the two remaining tattoos. One was perfectly circular, with alternating zigzagged and sloping lines bursting out from the center, like a sun drawn by a "creative" four-year-old child. The other was almost indescribable, a mixture of lines, dots, and overlapping triangles. I felt dizzy just looking at it.

"You got a preference, Bay?" Zo asked, finally coming out of the dressing room to get in on the tattoo action. My mouth dropped open. The little black dress was amazing, and the way it clung to her athletic frame looked almost sultry, in a little-bitty-blonde kind of way.

"Shut mouth," Zo told me with a half grin. If I'd been anyone else, she would have glared the flabbergasted look right off my face, but instead, she just nudged me. If Zo had one soft spot, it was me. "Pick a tattoo, Bay."

I tried not to look back at the two remaining tattoos, but I couldn't keep my eyes off the sunburst.

"I," Delia said, giving Zo's dress a once-over, "am a genius."

"You like the sun one." Zo interpreted my shrug and ignored Delia completely.

"Do you mind if I take it?" I asked.

"Mind?" she repeated. "Of course not. Do I look like a sunshine girl to you?"

With the contrast between the black dress and her mop of bright hair, Zo *did* look sunny. In fact, except for the wry expression on her face, she looked like Sunny McSunshine, but I wasn't about to tell her that.

"No," I said as I cut the last two tattoos apart. "You're not sunny."

"Amen to that," Delia added. "Now let's put these babies on. I'm putting mine on my stomach. With a little midriff showing, it'll be totally hot. Just a taste of the forbidden." She looked in the three-way mirror, admiring the belly-showing top she'd selected for her own dance attire.

"No way mine's going on my stomach," Zo said.

Annabelle wrapped her arms protectively around her waist, and Delia sighed, every inch the fashion martyr.

"I think I'll put mine on the nape of my neck," Annabelle said, sweeping her light brown hair over her shoulder. "That way, I'll know it's there, but no one else has to."

"What about you guys? Bay? Zo?" Delia looked from Zo back to me.

Zo looked almost comically horrified at the girlyness of the whole situation, and I just stared back at Delia, completely at a loss. I didn't have a clue where to put

2 1

my tattoo or, for that matter, how to get a guy (or The Guy) to go with me to the dance on Monday. Why was it that being a girl came so naturally to some people (*cough*, Delia, *cough cough*), and yet I didn't know the first thing about it?

"Your lower back," Delia told me after a long moment, like an artist finally touched by her muse. "With that two-piece outfit, which, I must add, was yet another stroke of genius on my part, it'll be divine. Not quite as obvious as the stomach, but still sexy. Mysterious, even."

"That's our Bailey," Zo said. "One giant mystery."

I smacked her in the stomach. "Nice dress," I told her. "Very sunny." She barely even noticed.

"So where are you sticking yours?" I asked, folding my arms over my chest.

Zo didn't falter for a second, and even though I knew her well enough to know that she hadn't decided until the minute I asked, she replied with all the certainty in the world: "I'm putting mine on my foot."

"Your foot," Delia repeated dully.

Zo nodded.

"Your foot?" Annabelle asked, a smile tugging on the edge of her lips.

Zo nodded again. "Yup," she said. "The top of my foot."

Delia spent about two seconds rolling her eyes and then turned her attention to her own midriff in the three-way mirror. "What do the instructions say about

22

applying?" she asked, holding the tattoo near her belly button. "I think these things usually need water or something." As the words left her mouth, Delia's hand pressed quickly to her stomach, and the tattoo, as if being sucked inward by a vacuum cleaner, moved swiftly toward her navel.

Delia looked down with a shrug. "I guess I figured out how to work it," she said. I didn't respond. Instead I stared at Delia's stomach, at the green almost half-butterfly. For a split second, the lines moved and swirled on their own, the blue-green color deepening until it was almost black.

Blood of the Sidhe.

The words echoed in my head. In the next instant, they were gone, and Delia was peeling her hand back from her stomach to reveal a glittering, nearly black tattoo.

"Perfect," Delia said, satisfied. Then she saw me staring at her. "Something wrong, Bay?"

As I stared at her stomach, I saw the black color of her tattoo flash in a burst of light, and in the next instant, the color morphed back to the blue-green it had been in the package. The light faded, and I heard Delia calling my name.

I tore my eyes away from her tattoo and glanced at Annabelle and Zo. Neither of them had seen a thing.

"Your turn, Bailey," Delia pronounced. "You wanted it on your back, right?"

I opened my mouth to answer, but no words came

out, and as I stood there, trying to remember what the whispering voice in my head had said, Delia took my silence as permission to pluck the tattoo from my hands, lift up the shirt she'd selected for me, and carefully arrange the sunburst on my back.

The moment it touched my skin, the room exploded into color. Blue, green, black, fuchsia, and the brightest yellow I'd ever seen. The colors swirled and throbbed, and I felt an ice cube run down my spine, followed by an incredible burst of heat from my lower back. Voices flooded the air, and the world around me fell into slow motion, a blur of colors that I couldn't quite make shapes out of.

To fight, to live . . .

The words repeated themselves over and over again in my head, spoken by two voices at once. The first was deep, and my body ached with the sound of it. The second, softer and feminine, soothed the ache but sent the world around me spinning as the voices melted into some kind of chant. I heard it behind me and around me. Inside of me. Cool and soothing, deep and dark, the voices pressed against my mind.

To fight, to live
We two of three bestow this gift
To see, to feel
To stand upon the ancient Seal
To know, to feed
To change, l'Sídhe

From earth she comes
From air she breathes
From water, her prison beneath the seas
Fire burn
Desire bleed
As we will, so mote it be.

The colors around me bled into one another, and with a burst of light, they and the voices were gone. The silence was heavy in the air, and with no warning, the entire world went black, and then there was nothing.

Chapter 3

"Your hair looks like moonlight."

I looked deep into Kane's eyes, blue offset by a fringe of dark lashes.

My entire body tingled as I looked up at him, barely able to believe that this was happening, that this was real. I was Bailey Morgan, background girl, and he was looking at me the way normal guys looked at Delia.

He rested his arms gently on my waist, encircling my hips.

"Moonlight?" I murmured softly. No one had ever compared my hair to moonlight. No one had ever compared my hair to anything, except for this kid named Randy Vinelli who had told me when we were four that it looked like a dead squirrel.

"Moonlight," Kane repeated, and with gentle fingers, he brushed my hair out of my face.

We swayed back and forth, his arms around my waist and mine on his shoulders, looking into each other's eyes and saying nothing.

"I've wanted this for so long," I whispered into his chest. Five years to be exact.

"I know." Kane's voice melted into a lilting accent that I didn't recognize, and when I looked up, he was gone.

He'd told me my hair looked like moonlight, and now he was gone. Biting my bottom lip, I glanced down at the hair on my shoulder. It sparkled in the light of the dance floor, every trace of my normal brownish blond, not-blond, not-brown color replaced by deep, shining silver.

"Is she all right? Maybe one of you girls should pour a little water on her."

"Bailey? Can you hear me, Bay?" Zo's voice broke into my mind, and my vision of the silver hair began to disintegrate.

"Try pinching her."

"I don't think—" Annabelle started to say, but the other voice cut her off.

"Just slap her cheeks lightly, and—"

"Hey! Back off, Barbie."

I opened my eyes to see Zo glaring at a big-breasted Escape salesgirl.

"Are you okay, Bay?" Delia asked me, the words pouring out of her mouth at warp speed. "One second you were fine, and the next, boom, you're going all googly-eyed and then you're lying on the ground, and you wouldn't wake up, and we went for help, and—"

"And then," Zo interrupted, totally in lioness-protecting-her-cub mode, "Push-up Bra Barbie over there wanted to smack you around a little to wake you up." She jerked her head toward the salesgirl, who was suddenly overcome with a need to go rearrange the buy-one-get-one-free jewelry.

"Is your outfit okay?" Delia asked the second the salesgirl was out of earshot.

"Are *you* okay?" Annabelle corrected firmly.

"I already asked that," Delia replied immediately. "And I can already tell she's fine." Delia dismissed the question with a wave of her hand. "Your skirt's not rumpled or torn or anything, is it?"

I looked down. For a split second, I saw myself as I'd looked dancing with Kane: moonlit hair, pearly skin.

She comes.

The words came unbidden into my mind and echoed like a tuneless song stuck on Repeat.

She comes. She comes. To fight, to live, she comes.

"Damn, Bailey," Zo said, breaking me out of the incessant chorus in my head. "You fainted from the pain of a fake tattoo. What's up with that?"

As soon as the word "tattoo" left her mouth, I

bolted straight up, and my hand flew to the small of my back.

"It looks great," Delia told me, folding her arms over her chest. "Perfectly positioned if I do say so myself."

I stood up, struggling to see the tattoo in the three-way mirror. There, in the middle of my back, it sat, like a sun rising out of my pants.

I shook my head to clear it of funky metaphors.

"You don't like it?" Delia asked, disappointed.

I opened my mouth and then closed it again. What was I supposed to say? That the tattoo had made voices in my head talk to me and the colors of the wind blur?

Instead, I looked at Zo and Annabelle. "Don't put yours on," I said. "I think these things might be . . ." I trailed off, looking for the right word. "I think they might be defective or something."

"Too late. Check out the girly goodness." Zo held out her foot.

Without a word, I turned to Annabelle. Knowing what I was thinking, she swept her hair back, and I saw the tiny intersecting crescents nestled in the nape of her neck, a brilliant blue-green against her pale white skin.

"When did you guys do that?" I asked them, my mouth dry.

"Same time you did," Zo answered, giving me a strange look.

"Did you . . ." I paused and glanced away. "Did anything weird happen when you put the tattoo on?"

"Yeah," Zo said, and I practically sighed in relief. "I realized that I was letting Delia accessorize me, and I had a compelling urge to chop off my foot," Zo continued.

"Like all the accessories in the world could turn you into a girl," Delia shot back, but there was laughter in her voice. They'd had this "argument" maybe a million times.

"So nothing strange happened?" I prodded.

"Like what?" Annabelle asked, examining my facial expression carefully.

"I don't know," I said, completely aware that I was the world's worst liar. "You didn't hear any voices or see or feel anything strange?"

All three of them stared at me blankly.

"All righty then," I said, glancing away. Maybe I really was going crazy. Since they were still staring at me, I did my best to pull off a smooth subject change. "I must just be a little light-headed is all," I said. "Maybe I need something to eat. Ice cream?"

"We just ate," Delia said, at the exact same time that Zo spoke up with a huge grin on her face: "Thought you'd never ask."

Delia cast a longing glance at the sale rack, and Annabelle looked at me, her eyes searching, before she glanced back down at her own feet.

"Maybe we should," she said, lifting her eyes to meet Delia's. "Get Bailey some food, I mean." She shifted her gaze back to me. Annabelle had a way of watching people that was subtle if you weren't looking for it, but I knew her well enough to know when she'd gone into observant mode—right now, she totally knew something was up. She just hadn't figured out what yet.

She comes. She comes. To fight, to live, she comes.

I heard the words, and I didn't. They were there in my head, whispered into the back of my mind over and over again, but somehow, I couldn't quite process what they were saying.

"Come on," Zo said, standing up with a grimace. Now that ice cream had entered the picture, she was all business. "If I don't get out of this dress pretty soon, I may have to hurt someone."

Delia narrowed her eyes at Zo. "Did I ever tell you that you have absolutely no vision whatsoever?" she asked. "Because you don't."

"Just change your clothes," Zo ordered, "so that the next diva wearing a lime green corduroy mini-whatever that passes by can use your room to try on her size-two hot pants."

"A corduroy lime green mini?" Delia huffed as she went back to her own dressing room. "Now *that* would be a travesty."

Annabelle stifled a grin at Delia's overdramatic tone, but kept her brown eyes locked onto mine, searching.

Ready for an escape, I slipped back into my dressing room, my head still ringing with words that I couldn't grasp and the image of Kane, his hands on my hips, still fresh in my mind.

"Finally," Zo said five minutes later when the rest of us had finished paying. "Let's—"

31

"Do you have this in a size two? This four is just waaaaaay too big."

The high-pitched, look-at-me-look-at-me voice carried across the room, and the four of us turned in unison to look at the familiar redhead standing there. Alexandra Atkins was swimsuit-model thin with a super-sized chest and an attitude to match. She was also wearing a corduroy lime green miniskirt so short that any of the rest of us could have worn it as a headband.

Freaky, I thought. Delia was right. That skirt *was* a travesty.

Alex continued lamenting the fact that they didn't have the hot pants she was looking for in a "non-massive" size, and the rest of us attempted to stop our eyes from rolling out of our heads.

"I mean, hello, why would a size eight even *want* to wear these pants?" Alexandra huffed.

Hey! I thought. *I* was a size eight.

"Are you sure a four is the smallest size you have?" Alex pouted.

"Tell you what," Zo said, taking a step forward, her impulse control (or lack thereof) kicking in as she practically leaped to the salesgirl's rescue. "Go eat something," she told Alexandra loudly. "Anything."

"Excuse me?" Alex asked, her voice cold as she turned around, miffed that we'd interrupted her poor-me-I'm-a-size-two speech.

"Eat something," Zo said, enunciating the words. "Then maybe you'll be a size four, and you can try on the pants." This coming from Zo, who, despite the fact that she inhaled food the way most people took in air, was more or less a size negative two.

"Did I say you could talk to me?" Alex asked. "I don't think so. Why don't you and your . . ." The redhead trailed off when she saw Delia. "Dee-Dee," she squealed in that fake-sweet voice popular girls always use when they see each other outside of school. Delia and Alex knew each other just well enough for Alex to know that Delia didn't let anyone (except Zo) call her by a nickname.

"And these are your little friends," Alex said, like she couldn't reconcile the fact that Delia was friends with the rest of us, just because she was pretty and a cheerleader and . . . well . . . Delia.

"I guess Zo *is* kind of little," Delia admitted with a candid grin, responding to Alexandra's "little friends" comment without so much as batting an eyelash. "But then again, you'd probably kill to be a size zero, huh?" Delia's voice was so pleasant that it took a few seconds for Alex to process her words.

Girls like Alexandra Atkins made me sick, and as she and Delia batted back and forth, pretending to play nice, I couldn't help but notice the way Alex threw barbs haphazardly at the rest of us.

When she made a comment about Annabelle being "adorably antisocial," I opened my mouth to say something, anything in my friend's defense, but A-belle just shook her head with a kind of quiet dignity, and in response to the look in her eyes, I shut my mouth. I also reached out a hand to restrain Zo, who didn't respond very well to people insulting her cousin. As I stood there, literally holding Zo back and basically letting Alex say whatever she wanted, frustration built up inside me. My body warmed, the heat spreading outward from the small of my back in gentle, cycling waves, and a single wisp of gray smoke rose up from the carpet.

Blood of the Sidhe.

More words I didn't understand permeated my brain, my very skin buzzing with the sound of their rhythm.

"By the way, have you seen Kane?" Alex asked Delia as a kind of grand finale.

The way she said his name broke me out of my trancelike state. Kane and Alex? God, I hoped not.

Alex measured my reaction and then smiled. "Well," she said flippantly, not bothering to wait for an answer to her oh-so-strategic question. "Shopping calls."

Zo snorted very obviously. For some reason, I found that snort strangely comforting.

Alex, however, did not. "Some of us care about this kind of thing," she told Zo. "Not that you'd understand. Your sense of fashion is . . ."

"I'm waiting," Zo said, her voice challenging and unaffected. Zo would let Delia get away with insulting her fashion sense from now until the next millennium, but Alex wasn't Delia, and Zo hadn't forgotten that the perky girl had insulted Annabelle.

Alex narrowed her eyes. "Well, actually," she said lightly, "your sense of fashion is kind of motherless, you know?"

My entire body exploded in fury as I watched Zo absorb the comment, her chin thrust out. Heat spread down my neck and into my arms, racing along my spine. The hairs on the back of my neck stood up one by one, and a second wave of heat rolled out from the small of my back, where I'd applied the tattoo. Objectively, I knew that the heat should have burned me, but something about the way it pulsed through my body made me long for more. Sweet, burning anger. Heat.

The air sizzled, literally, and Alexandra Atkins's shoe burst into flames.

I watched in a daze as Alex started screaming; watched as Zo took a flying leap to tackle the popular girl and beat her foot against the ground; watched as the flame subsided almost as quickly as it had come; and the entire time I watched, the strange words repeated themselves over and over again in my head.

Blood of the Sidhe.

Alex, in shock, finally shut her mouth long enough to give Zo a chance to speak. Zo stood up and dusted her hands off, fighting an ecstatic grin and failing miserably. "Your foot's not on fire anymore," she said, beaming. "My work here is done."

I forced the jumble of foreign sounds out of my head and processed Zo's words. Alex's foot had been on fire. She'd mentioned Zo's mother, I'd gotten

35

angry, and then her shoe had exploded into flames for no apparent reason whatsoever. I tried not to remember the feeling of heat scouring through my body; tried not to think about the way my blood had turned to fire: intoxicating, surging fire; and all that time, I'd been thinking about Alex and what she'd said to Zo.

My lower back throbbed slightly, and in the back of my mind, I heard words I'd heard before, two voices speaking as one, terrible and wonderful to listen to at once.

Fire burn
Desire bleed
As we will, so mote it be.

Fire burn. As I stared at Alexandra, my hand went to my lower back. The tattoo was warm to the touch, and as my fingertips brushed over it, my head filled with new words.

It's in the blood. Things of power always are.

Great, I thought weakly, my ears ringing with this proclamation. Not only was I insane and quite possibly inadvertently homicidal, but now, apparently, there was going to be blood.

Annabelle looked at Alex. "Did it burn through the shoe?" she asked. Leave it to A-belle to make sure that Alex was okay, even after the "adorably antisocial" comment. "How's your foot?"

"How do you think my foot is?" Alexandra hissed,

clamoring to her feet. "It was *on fire,* that's how my foot is!"

Annabelle took a single step back. Instinctively, I reached out for Zo, who was a microsecond away from literally leaping to her cousin's defense. The last thing we needed right now was for Zo to shove aforementioned foot up Alex's . . .

"Let's go," I said, my mind echoing with the word "fire" and with the feeling and the power that had preceded it. We headed for the door, and Delia, who'd remained suspiciously quiet through the whole ordeal, looked sadly down at Alexandra's shoes as we left. "It's such a shame," she said on our way out the door. "Those were great shoes." Then, because she could never tell half of a fashion story, Delia continued: "But that green mini was travesty city."

I barely heard Delia's proclamation, lost in thought as I digested what had just happened, and trying not to look directly at Annabelle, who was staring at me with the strangest expression on her face.

As we walked toward the exit, my fingers found their way again to the tattoo on my back.

She comes.
To fight, to live.
It has begun.

Chapter 4

We decided to forget about the ice cream.

I didn't say anything the entire walk home, but with every step we took, I saw in my mind images of Alex's foot and the fire I was becoming more and more convinced I had started. The small of my back throbbed, and I pushed down the urge to reach back and touch my tattoo—every time I touched it, I was filled with questions I couldn't understand, let alone answer.

Who was coming? What had begun? Why did touching the tattoo feel mildly like sticking my finger in an open socket?

As we walked, Annabelle snuck looks at me, trying to figure out my thoughts from the look on my face, and since Zo had become uncharacteristically mute after the whole Alex debacle, Delia was forced to fill the silence by giving us the verbal Cliffs Notes of this month's *Cosmo.*

By the time we reached my room, I couldn't keep it all in any longer. I'd never in my life managed to keep a secret from my three best friends, and with the way Annabelle was looking at me, the little wheels in her mind turning, it was only a matter of time before she started asking the right probing questions to get me to spill this one.

"Ummm . . . guys?" That was a brilliant start. Where was I supposed to go from there? Ummm . . . guys, I think I might have fire powers, and I just used them against Miss I'm-So-Perky-and-My-Boobs-Are-Too?

"Bailey," Annabelle said, rolling her eyes. "That fire was not your fault. You didn't start it."

Delia and Zo stared at her.

"What are you talking about, A-belle?" Zo asked. "Like Bailey actually thinks she started that fire. Not that I wouldn't have totally approved, because honestly, I think that might have been one of the high points of my life so far."

Annabelle frowned, wrinkling her forehead. "Weren't you listening?" she asked Zo, genuinely confused. "Bailey just said that she thought she had fire powers and that she'd set Alexandra's foot on fire."

"Would you like a side of crazy with your Bailey-so-did-not-just-say-that?" Delia asked.

They were right. I hadn't said it. I'd thought it.

"She did say it," Annabelle insisted. "Just a minute ago."

"No, Annabelle," I said, "I didn't."

Annabelle stared at me as though I'd just told her I was planning on tie-dyeing my dachshund.

This so wasn't happening.

"What isn't happening?" Annabelle asked, truly baffled. "And why would anyone tie-dye a dachshund?"

My mouth dropped open.

Annabelle, I thought, *can you hear me?*

"That would be a yes."

Annabelle, watch my lips.

Annabelle turned to look at me.

Are they moving? I asked her silently. *Are my lips moving?*

Slowly, Annabelle shook her head.

Am I making any sound? I asked.

She shook her head again.

"Oh," she said finally. Most people would have been cursing like crazy, but all Annabelle had to say was a very restrained "oh." "I'm hearing your thoughts, aren't I?" she asked weakly.

"A-belle, you're starting to scare me."

"She really is hearing my thoughts, Zo," I said. "Just like I really did accidentally set Alexandra's shoe on fire. Something weird is going on here."

She comes. This time, it wasn't a voice speaking in my head. It was me, remembering the two words I couldn't manage to forget. Someone, something was coming.

40

The knowledge sat there in the back of my mind as Annabelle and Zo went back and forth.

"She doesn't believe us," Annabelle informed me. Then she turned back to her cousin. "Zo, think of a number between one and fifty million."

Annabelle paused for just a moment. "Chocolate," she said finally, her voice barely more than a whisper as she intercepted the thought from her cousin's head and the reality of the situation settled in. "Zo, that's not a number between one and fifty million."

Zo's mouth dropped open. "Trick question."

"Now do you believe us?" I asked.

"Two things," Zo said. "First, yes I believe you. Second, A-belle, if you don't stay out of my head, I'm going to have to hurt you."

Annabelle shrugged, completely unimpressed by Zo's empty threat.

"Am I the only one here who is like totally confused and more than a little bit wigged out?" Delia asked. "I mean, so Annabelle's all psychic, and you're all fire-y, Bay . . . the little freaky alarm inside my head that goes off when freaky stuff happens is going wild. This is just strange and . . ." Delia trailed off, looking for the right word.

"Freaky," Annabelle, Zo, and I supplied at once. Delia nodded.

"Things like this don't just happen," Delia said. "I mean, one minute Annabelle's a boring, run-of-the-mill genius who doesn't talk much and has an average fashion sense, and the next she's psychic. How does that work?"

"I'm not a genius," Annabelle said automatically. For a second, I wondered at the fact that she hadn't objected to being called boring, but I had bigger things to think about.

"I think I know how it works," I said. "Or at least, I know when it started."

How to explain it to them? The feeling I'd gotten from the tattoo package. The way the air had morphed when Delia had applied her tattoo. The surging heat and the dizziness when they'd applied mine, and the voices . . . how was I supposed to explain the voices I'd been hearing and the words they'd said? Fire burning, someone coming, desire bleeding, Sídhe green. How did a person explain all of that, especially when it was becoming harder to remember any of it by the second?

"You explain slowly," Annabelle said, taking pity on me and going into scholarly Annabelle mode, "and possibly with charts." As quiet as she was the rest of the time, when it came to something that required organization of knowledge, Annabelle lit up like a Christmas tree.

Zo groaned. "I hate charts."

Annabelle paused for a moment. "I guess we don't *have* to have charts," she said in an almost comically sad voice. A-belle talked about charts the same way Delia talked about nail polish. "But Bailey's thoughts are just so complicated that I thought maybe . . . you know . . . charts might help."

42

I was about to take pity on her and say we could have charts when the implications of what she was saying hit me. Annabelle was psychic, and in my wondering how to tell them everything that had happened to me since applying that stupid tattoo, she'd caught it all.

Annabelle took a deep breath. "It all started," she said solemnly, still mourning the sacrifice of the charts, "with the tattoos."

Annabelle told them everything. It was the most I'd ever heard her say in one sitting, and when she finished, she gave in to the urge to grab some paper off my desk and started taking notes on what she'd said. I leaned forward to try to read what she was writing, but couldn't make out a single word.

There was a distinct chance she was making graphs.

"What I want to know," Zo said, "is why you're fire woman, and chart girl over there"—Zo jerked her head toward Annabelle, who appeared to be color-coding something—"is Little Miss Psychic, and Delia and I got a whole lot of nothing. I mean, we put on tattoos, too." Zo, leaning back on my bed, held up her bare foot and dangled it in front of me.

I stared at her tattoo for a moment, the blue-green color jumping out at me as if it had been made of pure, bright light.

Silver-blond hair. Blood. Dead, blue eyes.
It has begun.

43

"I don't know," I said, closing my eyes. My head pounded. Why was it that I was the only one who got dizzy just looking at the tattoos?

"I don't know," Annabelle said, answering my silent question and consulting her notes. "It could have something to do with the fact that you're the one who actually bought the tattoos. They were yours, and you just shared them with us."

"Like the tattoos know who owns them," Delia said skeptically.

"This from the girl who insists that her shoes would hate being worn by anyone else," Zo said. I opened my eyes just in time to see Delia launch a pillow at Zo.

"Hey, a girl's shoes are sacred."

The word echoed in my head for a moment.

Sacred.

"Maybe," Annabelle said, lifting the thought out of my head before I'd even put it into words. "Maybe there is something sacrosanct about the tattoos."

I wasn't surprised that my thoughts sounded smarter when Annabelle said them. When she'd moved back to the U.S. in the seventh grade, she'd used such big words that the rest of us hadn't been able to understand her. We figured it out eventually.

That was when Annabelle had stopped talking to anyone but us.

Delia flipped her hair behind her shoulder. "As great as this superpower talk really is, I think we have some other issues to deal with, like the fact that this Mango

Mermaid polish really needs three coats to achieve the tone I'm looking for."

Some people panic in a crisis. Delia painted her nails.

"Or maybe I could frost them," Delia said. "If I paint over them with a thin coat of Misty Madness . . ." She brushed one hand over the fingertips on the other, lost in her musings on the perfect nail.

No one but me saw the flash of blue-green light from Delia's stomach.

To fight, to live
We two of three bestow this gift. . . .

I shook my head to clear it of the now-familiar words.

Delia gawked at her hand. After a moment, she spoke. "Wow. Just wow."

"What?" Zo, Annabelle, and I asked at once.

Delia held up her right hand. "Notice anything different?" she asked.

The hand looked normal to me.

"Your 'wow, just wow' has something to do with your nails?" Zo flopped back down on the bed.

Delia held her other hand up next to it. Even from where I was standing, I could see that the nails on her right hand were a different color from the nails on her left. "Slightly frosted," Delia said in a shaky voice. "Like I just painted over them with Misty Madness."

"Can you do it again?" Annabelle asked, her pen flying rapidly over the paper as she spoke. "Can you change the color of the other nails?"

Delia ran her right hand over her left. "Misty Madness," she said out loud. Again, I saw the faintest hint of blue-green light roll in a wave off the tattoo on her stomach, and Delia beamed as she held up her newly frosted left hand.

"This," she said, "is so cool."

"So," I said slowly, "I have the power to start fires, Annabelle's psychic, and Delia can change her nail polish color just by running her hand over it?" Something about that last power didn't seem quite right.

"Maybe it's not just the nail polish color," Delia said. "Maybe it's any color." With a grin, she held her hands up to her head and ran them both down her hair. "Blond," she said, and as her hands passed over her thick locks, the hair turned blond, from the roots down.

Delia turned to look in the mirror. "This is so not me," she said, and the next instant, she was changing herself back.

Without a word, Annabelle walked over to my computer and turned it on.

"What are you doing?" I asked her.

"I'm going to try to find out what sort of telekinetic power would allow Delia to change something from one color to another," she said simply, as though this was the kind of thing she did every day.

"Telekinetic?" I asked. Just because Annabelle could

see into my head didn't mean I could see into hers, and I was having trouble following her, which freaked me out, since I considered myself completely fluent (or close to it) in Annabelle—gestures, big words, and all.

"A mental power," Annabelle explained as her fingers flew over the keys. "I can use my mind to read the minds of other people. Bailey, you can use your mind to start fires, and Delia can use hers to change colors and . . ." Annabelle glanced at Zo with an apologetic smile. "I'm sure your mind does something," she told Zo.

I bit back a smile. Zo picked up the pillow Delia had tossed at her and with artistlike precision, sent it flying into the side of Annabelle's head. Annabelle rolled her eyes. "I didn't mean it that way," she said. "You don't have to be so sensitive."

Zo? Sensitive?

"Yeah, right," Zo said, and then she wrinkled her forehead and continued speaking. "I'm sorry, cousin," she said in a muted voice. "That was inappropriate and uncalled for."

Zo looked down at her shoes, and Delia, Annabelle, and I all stopped what we were doing and stared at her.

"Inappropriate?" I asked. Since when had anything been inappropriate in the world of Zo?

"Cousin?" Delia squeaked. "Since when do you call Annabelle *cousin*?"

"I so did not just say that," Zo said. "Why in the world would I say that?"

"You even had a little Annabelle tone to your voice," Delia said. "Totally weird."

As soon as the words left Delia's mouth, silence fell over the room.

Zo had spoken with Annabelle's quiet, understated tones.

"You!" Zo said, pointing a finger at her cousin. "You put those words in my mouth, didn't you? How did you do that?" Zo glared at Annabelle. "I knew I'd never call you cousin on my own."

"I didn't mean to," Annabelle said meekly. "Honestly, Zo, I didn't. I didn't even know I could."

"It's okay," Zo said, softening her tone at the look on her cousin's face. "You didn't mean to, and I did overreact a tad bit."

I stared first at Annabelle and then at Zo. "Tad bit?"

"Damn it, A-belle," Zo yelled, somewhere between reluctantly amused and thoroughly exasperated. "Stay out of my head."

Annabelle sat there for a few seconds, saying nothing. "I'm not sure I can," she said finally. "But I'll try."

I looked at Annabelle, and a silent communication passed between us. I hadn't meant to set Alexandra's shoe on fire. Annabelle hadn't meant to put her words in Zo's mouth, just like she didn't mean to eavesdrop on every conversation I had with myself inside my head.

To fight, to live
We two of three bestow this gift. . . .

48

"Two of what three?" I muttered out loud, trying to forget the words I couldn't help but remember.

No answer.

Meanwhile, Delia was having a great time with her newfound power. "Do I want to wear mocha or pearl?" she mused under her breath. With a swipe of her hand, her fashionable white shirt darkened to a creamy light brown. Delia brought her hand back down, and the shirt turned white again, with just a bit of shine. Back and forth her hand went as she debated. "Mocha or pearl? Mocha or pearl?"

" 'Transmogrification,' " Annabelle said out loud, reading the word off my computer screen. " 'The ability to transform one type of matter into another type of matter.' " She paused. "If I'm reading this right," she said, wrinkling her forehead, "if Delia has transmogrification, then she should be able to change surface characteristics, like color, but she should also be able to change the form itself."

"Turn one thing into another?" Zo asked. She stared morosely down at her foot. "Stupid foot tattoo," she muttered. "Delia can change stuff, and I've got a whole lot of nothing."

"Hold on for just one second," Delia instructed. "Are you telling me that I could just wave my hands over, I don't know, a piece of paper and turn it into a Coach purse?"

"There's a chance that your power is limited simply to color," Annabelle said, still totally in academic, chart-making mode, "but I haven't come across any such—"

Delia cut her off. "This is officially the best day of my life," she said. Without another word, she charged over to my trash can and picked up a gum wrapper. "Baby blue cashmere socks," she said, running her other hand over it. Blue-green light surged out of her palm, wrapping itself around the wrapper, vibrating with words that only I could hear.

To know, to feed
To change, l'Sidhe

The next thing I knew, Delia was holding a pair of baby blue cashmere socks. "I love my life," she said. "Anyone else want anything? I think I'm going to make myself a dress like the one Nicole Kidman wore to the Oscars last year."

"Maybe you shouldn't," Annabelle said, biting her lower lip. "What if there's a side effect we don't know about?"

"You have got to be completely insane," Delia said. "I've got the magic touch, and there's no way I'm not going to use it. The way I see it, the fashion gods are smiling down on me."

Delia turned back to the trash can, and an instant later, she collapsed on the ground.

"Delia!"

"Just a little dizzy," Delia said, rolling over onto her back. "That's all."

"You feel like you've run a marathon," Annabelle said, tilting her head to the side as she lifted the thoughts out of Delia's mind. "Using the power takes a lot out of you. Much more than mine does for me or Bailey's for her."

Delia curled up into a ball with her new cashmere socks (formerly a gum wrapper) still in her hand. "Totally worth it."

"That's what you say now," Zo said, "but when Bailey's mom comes in here and starts fussing because you look sickly, maybe those socks won't look so good."

"You're just bitter because your foot tattoo didn't pay off the way my girly stomach tattoo did," Delia said. Delia was never too tired to argue with Zo. "You can't stand the fact that I—"

Delia's words were cut off by a knock at the door.

"Come in," I said. Delia pulled her shirt down over her stomach to conceal the tattoo the second before my mother walked in.

"I just came to see if you girls wanted a snack before I go to bed," my mom said. She paused and looked down at Delia. "Are you feeling all right, sweetheart? You look a little pale."

Immediately, my eyes flew to Zo, and sure enough, the tattoo on her foot flashed like a strobe light in front of my eyes, leaving my ears ringing with words I'd heard before.

To see, to feel
To stand upon the ancient Seal

"That's it," I said the second my mom left. "To see."

"What's it?" Zo asked. "See what?"

"Your power," I said. "Remember the thing with the lime green miniskirt? I mean, what are the chances that Alex would be wearing a corduroy lime green miniskirt and wanting to try on a pair of hot pants right after you said somebody would?"

Delia looked like she was about to start calculating the fashion probability of that happening, so I plowed on before she could interrupt. "And then this thing with my mom. You knew she was coming."

" 'Premonition,' " Annabelle read off the website. " 'A precognitive power in which the seer knows or sees the future before it occurs.' "

"That's it?" Zo asked. "Annabelle does her funky mind control thing, Delia can turn trash into jewels, Bailey sets stuff on fire, and I sometimes know some little insignificant event is going to happen before it does?"

For a moment, we were all silent.

Why? I thought. Why could we do these things? Who was coming? What had begun? Even without touching the tattoo or remembering what I'd heard, I couldn't banish the questions.

"This sucks," Zo said. "Why couldn't I have been the one with the fire?"

"Impulse control?" Annabelle suggested. She shuddered, and I couldn't tell whether she was joking or not. "It's probably a good thing that Bailey's the one with pyrokinesis."

"Pyrokinesis," I repeated, remembering the feel of flames surging through my blood.

"Sure," Zo said, "rub it in. And you probably won't even set the trash can on fire."

"Don't set the trash on fire," Delia said immediately. "Do you know how many pairs of shoes I could make out of the contents of that trash can?"

"Trust me," I told Zo. "You're the lucky one. I mean, I actually set someone on fire, Annabelle could probably make someone walk in front of a moving car if she wanted to, or make them say something awful to someone, or who knows what else, without even meaning to, Delia's probably going to transmogrify herself right into a coma, and we don't even know what's going on."

Annabelle's eyes widened. Apparently, she hadn't even thought that perhaps her mind control powers weren't limited to speech.

Delia yawned. "It's a definite possibility," she admitted sleepily in reference to my coma comment. "But I'll be the best-dressed comatose person you've ever seen."

Annabelle flipped through the notes she'd made, cross-referencing a couple of the pages. "You're right, Bay," she said finally. "We don't know why or what we're supposed to do or how we can keep from hurting people. All we know is that this all somehow goes back to the tattoos and to the two voices you keep hearing."

"So what do we do?" I voiced the question that everyone in the room was thinking.

"First off, you should write down everything you hear, Bailey," Annabelle said. Now that we were in her domain, she was more than happy to take charge.

More charts. I could practically see Zo thinking the same thing, and with her new psychic powers, Annabelle had to have heard us both, but she plowed on. "Tomorrow, we go directly to the source."

The rest of us looked at one another. What source?

"The woman who sold us the tattoos," Annabelle said, jotting one final note down in the margins of her paper. "If anyone knows anything about the tattoos, it would have to be her."

Delia sat up. "You know what that means, don't you?" she asked, a gargantuan grin spreading across her face.

"What?" I asked.

"Tomorrow morning, we're going back to the mall."

Chapter 5

That night marked a first among our Friday-night sleepovers. I was normally the first or second one out, but that night, while everyone else slept, I stared up at the ceiling from my sleeping bag on the floor. What if whoever was "coming" came while we were sleeping? What if I had a nightmare and burned the house down? For that matter, what if Delia turned the whole house and all of us into some kind of massive Jimmy Choo? For all I knew, Annabelle, who was asleep on the floor next to me, might well be in the process of unintentionally turning the whole neighborhood into zombies who said things with muted voices while staring at their shoes.

"Isn't it fabulous?" Delia murmured into her pillow. She was an infamous sleeptalker. "*Très* chic."

My eyelids drooped, and I rolled over onto my side, telling myself sternly to keep my eyes open. Until I got a handle on this fire thing, I was determined not to fall asleep.

So, of course, thirty seconds later, I fell asleep.

I heard the waterfall before I saw anything. The air hummed with it, the sound of water falling on stone saturating the silence of the room. I opened my eyes and realized that I didn't remember closing them. I stared up at the ceiling. Not my ceiling. There was water flowing there, from one side of the ceiling to the other, and then down the walls and onto the floor. My hands went to grab my sleeping bag to pull it over my eyes, but instead, they hit cold stone. I sat up and realized that I wasn't in a sleeping bag at all and that, given the freaky overhead waterfall thingy, that shouldn't have come as a surprise.

I ran my hand over the stone beneath me. Its surface was smooth, but every so often, my hand would run across some kind of indentation. It took me a moment to realize that something had been carved into this stone. I stood up and backed away, anxious to get a look at the whole thing. It was round and raised slightly above the rest of the floor. As I backed off the stone carving, I felt grass underneath my feet; wet grass on a pleasantly warm summer day.

"It's always summer here, when we wish it to be summer."

That voice. I knew that voice. Feminine and soft, but so powerful. So old.

56

The owner of the voice laughed. "No lady likes to be told that she's old, child," she chided.

I squeezed my eyes shut. This was not happening.

"Not even an immortal lady," a second voice added. This one was low and deep, and no less horrible or less wonderful than the first.

"Immortal?" I squeaked, and then I cursed myself. My eyes were closed, I was trying to convince myself that this wasn't happening, and yet I talk to them? Brilliant.

"Look at us, child."

I didn't want to, but the voice was so beautiful, so awful, that I couldn't help myself. Slowly, I turned around, and after a deep breath, I opened my eyes.

The woman's hair was such a dark shade of red that I was only half sure it wasn't black. It fell in thick waves, past her shoulders and down to her waist, and it shined so much that had the room been pitch black, she could have lit the entire thing with the light of her hair.

The same kind of light came from her eyes, which were so blue I could barely stand to look at them.

The man beside her had hair darker than hers, black with a blue shine to it, and he had the same disarmingly blue eyes.

"Immortal?" I asked again, and a million other better questions ran through my head. Where was I? Why was I here? Who were they? Why did they keep talking to me? What did they want from me?

"Rest easy, child," the woman said, plucking my fears and questions from my head with ease. "We are not here to harm you. You are safe in this place. For thousands of your years, this place has remained pure and untarnished by violence. For now, it is safe."

She gestured to the round, carved stone on the floor.

"The Seal," she said softly. "It protects this place from those who would do it, and your world, harm."

This chick was saying "harm" just enough to make me nervous.

She stepped forward and took my hand in hers. Her skin was soft and slightly cool, like the stone seal itself. "I am Adea," she said. "He is Valgius. We must speak quickly. We cannot bring our world into your dreams for long.

"To answer your questions: We are not immortal. Someday, hundreds of thousands of your years from now, we will grow old. We could die before then should great harm come to us or the balance, and through the balance, the Seal, but we have lived for tens of thousands of your years. To you, our life span may seem immortal, but that is simply your word for a very long time.

"You're here because we've brought you and because you brought yourself. You are here because of the blood."

"Sidhe blood," I blurted out, remembering their voices in my head when I'd first seen the tattoos.

"We are Sidhe," the man said simply. "And we need your help."

And just like that, the dream was gone, and I was staring up at my ceiling, my forehead drenched in sweat and the tattoo on my back throbbing as if someone had stuck a knife into it.

"Breathe, Bailey," I told myself. "Just breathe."

Easier said than done. The echo of the man's voice in my head was so loud, so overpowering, that nothing, not even the need for oxygen, could overcome it.

We are Sídhe, and we need your help.

"Shee," I said out loud, trying to match the way the slightly accented voice in my head pronounced the foreign word. "Sheeeeee."

"Bailey?" Annabelle sat up in her sleeping bag and looked at me, her brown hair mussed and her eyes sleepy. She paused, waiting patiently for me to fill her in.

"Don't you know?" I asked. "I mean, can't you do your . . ." I made wiggly finger motions next to my forehead. "Can't you do your psychic thing and just lift it from my head?"

Annabelle wrinkled her forehead slightly and stared at me with solemn brown eyes. "I can't see anything. Something about a dream, but that's all I'm getting." She paused. "You know, I don't think I ever knew exactly what you remembered the voices saying. I only ever got your thoughts on what they had said." Pulling her legs to her chest, she laid her chin on her knees. "It's like I'm one step removed," she said. "I can't access anything directly about the voices, only that they scared you and that you're confused." She reached and touched my hand lightly.

Finally remembering to breathe, I exhaled and blew

my hair out of my face. "Scared and confused is a total understatement," I said. "I had this dream, and . . ."

As Annabelle leaned forward to listen, she cast a quick but longing glance in the direction of the notes she'd made earlier that night.

"You want me to write it down, don't you?" I asked.

Biting her bottom lip and shooting me an apologetic look, she nodded sheepishly.

A bit light-headed and with my back still throbbing, I stood up and tiptoed around a sleeping Zo to get to my desk. After turning on my desk lamp, I grabbed a sheet of paper out of my printer and a pen out of the drawer and began writing down everything I remembered.

Adea, I wrote down. The woman's name stuck in my mind, and as I wrote it, I could hear her voice, gentle but commanding, serene but desperate. What was it about their voices? They were so . . .

So not human.

I scribbled down a really lame description of the woman's voice and her glowing black-red hair, and then I moved on to the man. What had Adea said his name was?

I closed my eyes, trying to remember. With a surge of pain from my lower back, the name came to me.

Valgius. I wrote it down and stared at it. Had I even spelled that right? Was it a *j* instead of a *g*? What kind of name was Valgius anyway?

I tapped my pen lightly on the desk. What else?

The Seal. When I'd opened my eyes in the dream,

I'd been sleeping on some sort of circular etched stone. Adea had called it the Seal, capital S, and she'd said something else about it. This time even my aching back didn't provide me with the answers. The dream was becoming foggier and foggier, and though I could picture the waterfall overhead and Adea's painfully blue eyes perfectly, I was losing the rest of it quickly.

Adea had said I was safe there, something to do with the Seal. I scrawled this down onto the paper, feeling stupid for not remembering more. Finally, I added two last items to my makeshift journal entry.

"Blood of the Sídhe," I wrote, and seeing the word "Sídhe" written down surprised me. That was how you spelled it? And how did I know that? Had the knowledge just been shoved into my head with Adea's words? Or had I always known?

Always.

I shook my head and wrote one more thing.

"They need our help," I said aloud as I wrote. "Help doing what?" I glanced back over my shoulder at Annabelle.

She said nothing, and for a moment, I wished that I'd been given her power. Sometimes it was so hard to tell what Annabelle was thinking, and now she had a VIP pass into all our thoughts.

"I'm thinking that we can do this." A-belle obligingly filled me in. "Whatever it is they need help with, whoever it is that is coming. You, me, Delia, Zo . . . we can do this." She looked away for a moment and then

6 1

took the paper gently from my hands. Even though the only light was the moon shining through my window, Annabelle promptly began color-coding. I wasn't even sure how she'd found her highlighters in the dark.

"But what about the purple?" Delia said loudly on the bed, her eyes still closed.

Annabelle and I stifled a giggle. Delia was so going to hear about this in the morning.

"Goodnight, Bailey," Annabelle said, putting the paper away and squeezing my arm once before she lay back down in her sleeping bag.

"Night, A-belle."

For a long time after that, I lay there, curled up in my sleeping bag, listening to the sound of the blood pumping through my veins and the wind outside my window.

Know you, the wind howled. *Know you.*

I was so close to the edge of a dream that I could barely make out the words, and before I could wonder whether I was already dreaming or not, I fell into a deep sleep, the sound of the wind and my pounding heart fading into the background. My last conscious thought was to wonder why Adea and Valgius had said nothing about the mysterious "she," whoever she was, and why I had not thought until now to ask.

"Your hair looks like moonlight."
On some level, I knew I'd been here before, but his voice

was so low and sweet that I pushed the thought out of my mind and laid my head on his chest.

"Moonlight," Kane said again, and with gentle fingers, he brushed my hair out of my face. This time, I brought my hand up to touch his, and for the longest time, we just touched fingertips. Slowly, his hand worked its way down my arm, and then we were dancing.

We moved as one, our bodies close together, swaying to music that I almost recognized.

"I've wanted this for so long," I told him softly. I almost couldn't remember ever wanting anything else.

This time, he moved his hand to my face and tucked a strand of my hair behind my ear.

"I know," he said. "Know you." He moved his lips toward mine, and when he spoke again, I could feel his breath on my face. "I've always known you."

And then, he was gone.

Chapter 6

"I'm telling you, Bay. We've got four permits. Five if you count the fact that I have two because my first picture was so hideous that I told them I lost it and got another one. Five permits . . . that's like two and a half licenses. At least."

I stared back at Delia. She couldn't honestly believe that I'd let her drive my mom's car, could she?

"I doubt it," Annabelle said, answering my unasked question.

"You doubt what?" Zo asked suspiciously. "I wish you two would stop it with the silent talking." Zo was still a little bit grumpy that I could set things on fire and she just got vague feelings about lime green miniskirts.

"Delia, you're not taking my mom's car anywhere.

We're not taking my mom's car anywhere. We either walk or we catch a bus, but we're not driving to the mall."

Delia snapped her fingers. "Silly me," she said. "Did I forget to tell you that I got my license? It's in here somewhere. . . ." She fiddled around in her purse. After a few seconds, she bit her bottom lip, and green light filled the purse. "Here we go," she said, handing me her permit, or at least handing me the item that had been her permit five seconds ago, before she'd done her little change-y mojo on it and turned it into a license.

"And you turned sixteen when?" Annabelle asked, a bemused expression on her otherwise serious face.

"A couple days ago." Delia laughed lightly. "You know me, I don't like to make much of a fuss about little things like birthdays."

"Four months and three days," Zo reminded her. Delia kept a running count of the days until her sixteenth birthday and had since she was eight.

"Two days," Delia corrected automatically. She sighed heavily. "It was worth a shot."

I wrinkled my forehead. There was no world in which any of us would have bought the fake license. The scary thing was, arguments like that worked for Delia all the time, no matter how ridiculous they were. Just not with us. Such was the glory of being Delia Cameron.

Delia's eyes sparkled with mischief. "Want me to turn your permit into a license?" she asked.

65

It was a very tempting offer. "Later," I said. "For now, we have to find a way to the mall."

Delia stuck out her lower lip in an exaggerated pout.

"Let's just walk," Zo said. "What's the good of living within walking distance of the mall if you don't actually walk to it every once in a while?"

"The feeling you get just from knowing the mall is close by," Annabelle said as the four of us grabbed our purses and made our way out the front door. Zo and I stared at Annabelle. "Delia's answer, not mine," Annabelle clarified.

"I had a dream last night," I blurted out as we made our way across the street. Something about being around the three of them made me want to spill my guts and then some.

"A Kane dream?" Delia asked knowingly. "Was he hot? What were you wearing?"

"No, not a Kane dream," I said. I could feel the goofy grin spreading over my face just from saying Kane's name. "Well, I actually did have one of those, too, but that wasn't the dream I was talking about." I glanced over at Annabelle. "I dreamed about the voices I've been hearing."

Even though I knew they believed me about everything, I still felt like I sounded absolutely nutso.

"I mean, I dreamed about the owners of the voices." I paused. "I think they're real."

Silence. Absolute silence.

We walked for a while before I spoke again. "They

said they needed our help. They didn't say why, but I think we have these powers because of them." It was all really fuzzy in my mind, and it was getting so much fuzzier as I said it out loud that the inside of my mouth practically felt as if it was growing fur.

"Do they have names?" Annabelle asked, always the one to ask the right questions at the right times.

"Adea," I said. "And Valgius."

"Why are you whispering?" Zo asked me dryly. "Is it top secret?"

I so wasn't in the mood for sarcasm. "Don't make me set you on fire," I said.

Zo cracked a grin and snorted. "You wouldn't even set the trash can on fire," she said, slinging an arm around my shoulder. "That's why I love you."

We'd been friends for so long that sometimes I forgot Zo had a sweet side to her.

It only took her about five seconds after she'd slung her arm over my shoulder to slip me into a headlock. "Admit it," she ordered, laughing. "You love me, too."

Delia rolled her eyes.

I elbowed Zo in the stomach. In retaliation, she ruffled my hair.

"Watch out, Zo," Delia said, laughing despite herself, "Bailey bites." Annabelle and Zo lost it, and I made the mistake of giggling with hair in my face and ended up with a mouthful of hair.

"Huh," a voice I so didn't want to hear right now said. "Bailey bites?"

Zo let loose of me, and I straightened up and stared in horror at the owner of the voice.

Your hair looks like moonlight.

Kane sat behind the wheel of his black SUV, looking down at us with his perfectly gorgeous eyes.

Why was it that whenever Kane saw me in real life, I was always stuck in some kind of awkward position? In the past twenty-four hours, he'd seen me sprawled across the ground and in a headlock, choking on my own hair.

And now he thought I bit people. It was official. The love gods hated me. And wanted me to suffer. And . . .

"Don't worry, Kane," Delia said with a wicked grin. "Bailey doesn't bite *hard*."

My mouth dropped open. "Delia," I hissed.

Kane laughed out loud. "I don't bite too hard, either," he said. He paused for a microsecond, staring at me, and my cheeks burned.

No burning! I thought frantically. The last thing I wanted to do was set Kane on fire. Somehow, I was pretty sure that would take playing hard to get a little too far. I breathed in, forcing my blush down.

"You ladies need a ride somewhere?" Kane asked.

"Hallelujah, he has a car," Delia said.

"We'd love a ride." Annabelle interpreted Delia's response.

Thirty seconds later, I was sitting in the front seat, with Delia, Annabelle, and Zo squeezed into the back behind us.

"Where you guys going?" Kane asked.

"The mall," I replied.

"Always a good choice," he said, and I couldn't decide whether he was making fun of us or being serious.

I opened my mouth and then closed it again. What was I supposed to say? He was Mr. Important, and I was Bailey, Queen of Nothing.

"Are you going to the dance on Monday?" Delia asked from the backseat. She never had any trouble talking to guys.

"Probably," Kane said.

"Bailey's probably going, too," Delia replied. She was clearly a girl on a mission.

I turned around in my seat and glared at her. First she makes me sound like I'm into biting people, and then she practically throws me at him? I was going to kill her. I was so going to kill her, and all that would remain would be a pile of designer clothes covered in Delia ashes.

I stared out the window, determined not to look Kane in the face. Obviously, he hadn't thought too much of Delia's proposition. We pulled up to the mall about two excruciating minutes later.

"Thank you for the ride," Annabelle said.

"We'll see you at the dance." Delia winked at Kane. "All of us," she added with a meaningful look in my direction.

Dead girl walking, I thought as I stepped out of his car.

"I'll see you," Kane mumbled. Delia gave him a hard look. "I'll see you at the dance," he corrected himself with a grin. "And Bailey?"

He'd actually gotten my name right. It was a miracle.

"Yeah?" It wasn't exactly a brilliant reply, but at least I managed to say something instead of just standing there staring at his gorgeous blue eyes. And the way a smile tugged at the edges of his lips when he looked at me. And . . .

"Save a dance for me."

Those words actually came out of his mouth.

"Okay," I said, completely unable to manage any multiple-word sentence.

"Okay," Kane repeated, and our eyes met for a second, caught up in another silent moment.

"I'll see you," he said.

"Yes."

"Yes?" Delia asked the instant Kane pulled away. "The guy you've been head over heels for since you were *eleven* says he'll see you and you say 'yes'?"

"I can't believe you did that!"

Delia gave me an innocent look. "What?"

"You practically threw me at him," I said.

"You can thank me later," Delia said. "For now, we have some serious tattoo business to deal with."

I would have smacked her, but since I was grinning like an idiot, I couldn't bring myself to do it. Kane wanted to dance with me.

Your hair looks like moonlight. I remembered my

dream. *Know you, know you.* Maybe I'd gotten a little bit of Zo's premonition along with my fire power.

"Why would you think you have premonition?" Annabelle asked me curiously.

I was starting to see Zo's point about the downfalls of this whole Annabelle-is-psychic thing.

"Just this dream I had," I said, surprised that she hadn't picked up on it. I'd barely thought of anything else all morning. "Never mind," I told her when she opened her mouth again. "It's not important."

The three of them stared at me, grinning.

"What?" I asked.

"Bailey's in lo-ove." Zo expertly made love into a two-syllable word.

"Shut up," I said, but I couldn't wipe the grin off my face. This wasn't love. Exactly. This was . . .

"Can we just do what we came here to do?" I said.

Delia hooked her arm through mine. "Bailey's right," she agreed.

I gave her a grateful look.

"We can talk about her love life later. Now, let's go." With the expertise of someone who could make it through the mall blindfolded faster than we mere mortals could with our eyes open, Delia navigated the way back to the stand where I'd bought the tattoos. When we got there, we saw a sign. CLOSED IN PREPARATION FOR MABON.

"Mabon?" Delia said. "What's Mabon? It sounds like a brand of makeup."

"It's a fancy name for the autumnal equinox," Annabelle said. We stared at her. How in the world did she know this stuff? Annabelle blushed. "I read it somewhere," she explained, and I had the distinct feeling that Mabon was a few minutes away from getting added into her handy-dandy color-coded notebook.

"Well, this sucks," Zo said, never one to sugarcoat things. "Now we're back where we started."

"Touch your tattoo, Bailey," Annabelle told me suddenly.

"Why?" I asked, but my hand was already moving. I looked at Annabelle, alarmed. "Are you moving my hand, or am I?"

Annabelle looked at me, stricken. "I—I don't know."

I shook my head to clear it and then let my fingertips graze the tattoo on the small of my back.

She comes. Angry, vengeful. She will stop at nothing to destroy us. She comes.

I repeated the words out loud to my friends.

"And who's this chick who's supposed to be coming?" Zo asked.

"I don't know," I said. "All I know is that whoever she is, she's been coming since yesterday afternoon. Right after we put the tattoos on, the little voices were all about 'she comes' and stuff." I closed my eyes, willing the voices to tell me more, but nothing came. "That's it," I said. "That's all I'm getting."

"Try touching the stand," Annabelle said. "Or the sign. If the person who sold the tattoos to us had something to do with this, maybe they left some kind of, I don't know, some kind of trace or something behind. Just run your fingers over everything and see if you hear anything."

It was kind of strange, but I was getting used to A-belle taking charge.

"But if the voices are really just Adea and Valgius talking to me," I whispered back, careful not to talk too loudly about the voices since I didn't want the entire mall to think I was crazy, "why don't they just tell me whatever it is they want me to know?"

Annabelle bit her bottom lip in thought. "Maybe they need some medium to speak to you through," she said. "Like the tattoo. Or like something else in or on this stand."

I thought for a moment, and then I ran my fingertips gently over the edge of the kiosk. Nothing. I touched the sign lightly, and as I touched the word "Mabon," the voices filled my head.

She comes, she comes. To fight, to live, she comes.

Same old, same old, I thought.

Our lives. Your fight. Both worlds.

I relayed the new information to the group, and they stared at me, waiting for more than a cryptic suggestion that we might have to fight for our lives sometime soon.

"Why can't someone else hear the freaky voices?" I

asked, feeling completely useless. "Why does it always have to be me?"

My friends didn't say anything. Zo ran her hand along the sign, and without warning, she gasped, her eyes rolling back in her head and blue-green light that I deeply suspected only I could see streaming out of her face.

"I guess someone else is hearing the freaky voices," I said, my voice shaking. "Big yay on that one."

"I don't think she's hearing anything," Annabelle corrected softly. "I think she's seeing something." Annabelle looked at me and swallowed hard. "Something bad."

"Zo?"

Zo didn't respond.

"Okay, now you're freaking me out," I said.

"Zo?" Delia's voice was uncharacteristically little. "Come on, babe, pull out of it."

With no warning, the light disappeared, and Zo fell forward onto the kiosk, gasping for air.

"What did you see?" Delia, Annabelle, and I all asked at once.

"A girl," Zo said. "Really blond hair. Like white. She was singing to herself under her breath, this freaky song that sounded like a mix of a lullaby, a death march, and some kind of twisted nineties boy band. She was standing on a balcony or something, and then her eyes just kind of glazed over, like she was seeing something the rest of us couldn't." Zo paused. "And she just stared at nothing, for the longest time, and then her eyes flashed, like they actually lit up and turned bright blue, and then her pupils disappeared, and I saw her leave her body."

"Leave her body?" I asked. Someone was sounding crazy, and for once, it wasn't me, but I couldn't be happy about it. Not with Zo standing there, looking as though she was about to burst into tears. Zo, who I'd seen cry a grand total of once since she was four.

"She just stepped out of it. I saw her body, and I saw her, and she wasn't in her body. And then something pulled her away, and she was gone, and her body was just standing there, and then the blue left her eyes, and her eyes closed." Zo swallowed hard, and I felt the hairs on the back of my neck stand up one by one. "And then," Zo continued, looking down at her shoes, her voice reduced to a whisper. "Then the body fell forward, off the balcony."

Zo looked up at us, and her voice hardened. "She was on the eleventh floor."

Her words sunk in, and I couldn't shake the image from my mind. The girl, standing by herself, singing, and then . . . boom, no more girl.

"Premonition," Annabelle said in her I-know-my-definitions voice, "is having visions of the future."

I squeezed Zo's shoulder. "So whatever you saw," I said, catching on to A-belle's point, "it hasn't happened yet."

"We can stop it," Delia said. When Delia said something in her confident voice, it was nearly impossible not to believe it.

"But what about the voices?" Annabelle asked softly. "You know: 'our fight, both worlds'?"

I shook my head, my eyes still locked on to Zo's. "That fight's just going to have to wait," I said. "Zo, do you have any idea where the girl was?"

Zo closed her eyes, her forehead wrinkling as she thought. "Near the beach," she said. "She could see the ocean from the balcony."

We lived in a beach town. That description described every hotel and about half the apartments in the whole city.

"You said she was on the eleventh floor," Delia said suddenly. "That leaves the Richmond and the Delux." Noticing the impressed look I was giving her, Delia shrugged. "What?" she said. "I can't be useful?"

"The Delux is on the other side of town," I said, referring to one of the nicer hotels in the area. "How in the world would we get there?"

Zo swallowed hard. "Let's hope it's the Richmond," she said. After that, she refused to say anything, and for the first time in the history of our little foursome's weekly shopping trips, Delia Cameron left the mall in a hurry, without buying anything, the rest of us on her heels.

Chapter 7

Even though it was the off-season, the Richmond was crawling with people, half of whom were wearing sunglasses and a good three of whom appeared to be standing near the front desk doing some form of yoga that involved chanting. Zo tore through the lobby, a girl on a mission, and the rest of us struggled to keep up. The second we stepped outside, Zo froze, her eyes locked on the ocean. The smell of the salt water hung in the air, and the waves crashed gently into the beach, the light sand darkened to brown by the water's touch.

From earth she comes
From air she breathes
From water, her prison beneath the seas

I looked at Zo, and then followed her gaze and stared back out at the ocean.

"This was what she was looking at," Zo said softly. "The ocean, and the way it had about a million different shades of blue and green in it, melding together with each wave." Zo paused. "There were people on the beach," she said, "playing volleyball." She wrinkled her nose in thought. "One of them hit the ball into the water, and the others threw him in."

Zo looked back at us, her voice caught in her throat.

I grabbed her hand and just held it.

"She wanted to be down there with them," she said. "She wanted them to forget about . . . about whatever it was she'd done. She felt bad about it, and she just wanted them to . . ."

Zo broke off. "There," she said, pointing to the building on our left.

The balconies were small, barely big enough for two people to stand comfortably. The wrought-iron railing was black, each balcony identical to the one next to it. And the one above it. And the one below it.

"How are we going to find her in time?" Zo asked. "She could be in any of those rooms, and if we wait until she goes out on the balcony . . . She's on the eleventh floor. We won't make it in time."

Delia swallowed hard. "What if we already haven't made it in time?" she asked with an uncharacteristic amount of tact in her voice. "It took us twenty minutes to walk here."

78

"People probably would have noticed a body falling eleven stories onto the ground below," Annabelle pointed out, always the voice of reason. She looked up, doing quick calculations in her mind. "There are only seven rooms on each floor that face the ocean, and we know it's the eleventh floor."

"Well, what are we waiting for?" Zo asked. "Let's get up there."

This time, Zo took off running, Delia right behind her like a champ. How in the world was she managing in heels? Annabelle and I were slower, and by the time we'd reached the building's entrance, Zo was already cursing heavily at the door.

"What's the matter?" I asked dumbly.

"Locked," Zo grunted between clenched teeth.

"I tried doing the change-y thing to this flier to make a key card," Delia said, "but I don't know what they look like, and it's not working."

"It makes sense," Annabelle said thoughtfully. "If you don't have a goal in mind, you can't transmogrify properly."

Zo opened her mouth (probably to say something she'd later regret), but Annabelle continued thinking out loud. "Instead of trying to transmogrify a key," she said, "maybe try to transmogrify the lock?"

Annabelle Porter: problem solver.

Delia held her hand over the lock. "Tapioca," she said. An instant later, pudding oozed down onto the floor, and Zo pulled the door open.

"Pudding?" she asked Delia.

"Tapioca pudding?" I echoed. "You could transmo-grify the lock into just about anything, and you chose tapioca pudding?"

Delia tossed her hair behind her shoulder. "Don't argue with success," she said. She tapped her foot impatiently. "Are we here to do the life saving thing or not?"

Zo made a beeline for the elevator, and we followed her. "Eleven," she said out loud, punching the button as soon as she stepped into the elevator. "Eleven, eleven, eleven."

"Zo, I don't think pushing it multiple times helps," I said.

"Neither does pushing it harder," Delia added.

"You didn't see her," Zo said fiercely. "You just . . . you didn't see her."

The elevator door closed, and we rode in silence. When the elevator stopped on the fourth floor, I thought Zo was going to explode.

"Sorry. No room," she yelled full-volume at the two teenage boys standing there when the door opened. One tried to step into the elevator, but Zo shoved him out hard enough that he hit the opposite wall. "No. Room."

"Was that entirely necessary?" Delia asked when the door closed again. "The one on the left was kind of cute."

"What if they'd been going to a floor under eleven?" Zo asked. "That's time we might not have—"

"Be quiet," Annabelle interrupted, force in her voice. "All of you. Be quiet now." Unused to hearing that tone from Annabelle, we obeyed, and A-belle closed her eyes.

"They'll never forgive me," she whispered softly. "I didn't mean to break their stupid circle, and now, they'll never forgive me."

"Annabelle?"

"Quiet!" Annabelle brought her right hand to her temple. "I don't see why we even have to come to these stupid things. Mom knows I hate them. I never asked to be a part of their circle, anyway. I never asked to be like this. . . ."

The arrow above the elevator door pointed to the numbers of the floors as we passed them. Eight. Nine.

Annabelle kept murmuring under her breath, someone else's words.

Ten.

"I just want . . . want . . ." Urgency unlike any I'd ever heard entered her voice: pure raw need. *"Want."*

Eleven.

"It's gone," Annabelle said, her eyes fluttering open. She stepped off the elevator onto the eleventh floor, and the rest of us followed her. "I can't hear her thoughts anymore."

"We're too late," I said, my stomach turning itself inside out with dread.

"No," Zo said forcefully, slamming her fist up against a window. She looked out and opened her mouth. "No," she said again, this time more softly. "Look. Down there, on the beach. That guy just hit the ball into the water. I've seen this before." Zo looked up at us. "We still have time."

She took off running and banged her fist against the first door she came to. "Don't just stand there," she said. "You guys take the other ones."

When a dark-haired man answered her door, Zo looked him straight in the eye. "Door check," she said. "Everything's fine."

Door check? That was the best she could come up with? Realizing that we didn't have time to lose, the rest of us joined in, each taking a door as Zo pounded furiously on her next.

No one answered my door, and I was about to turn to leave, when I heard the faint sound of humming.

Hadn't Zo said the girl was singing? Humming was close.

"Guys, I think she's in here."

"Delia," Zo barked out. "Lock. Tapioca. Whatever."

Delia ran over, her hands held out. "Butterscotch pudding," she yelled out.

When Zo yanked the door open, butterscotch pudding splattered onto my pant leg, but I wasn't exactly in the position to spend much time thinking about my favorite pair of jeans.

"There, on the balcony," Zo said. I could still hear the faint sound of humming. It grew louder with each step I took toward the balcony. There was something about the sound that just wasn't right, but I couldn't place my finger on it. When Zo threw open the sliding door, I stepped forward, tilting my head to the side.

Alone on the balcony stood a girl with white-blond hair staring straight ahead, her eyes locked on nothing at all. Without preamble, Zo stepped onto the balcony and shook her. The girl didn't respond.

The humming continued, and when I really listened to the sound, it hit me like a punch to the stomach. Except for Zo, the girl was alone, but I heard two voices humming. I squeezed out onto the balcony and in front of the girl, following her gaze.

I saw nothing, but when I turned back to look at the girl head-on, I stopped breathing.

A thin, almost smoky, cord was wrapped firmly around her body, extending out past the railing and into the air where the girl was staring. As I watched, another wispy string lashed out, wrapping itself around her waist.

What in the world was going on here?

One by one, the tiny, nearly transparent cords appeared, wrapping around the girl and encircling her like string-thin tentacles latching on to prey. I watched in horror as the strings passed one another, moving in a dreadful, purposeful dance. Within seconds, thousands of the strings were weaving themselves together, creating a net behind the girl.

And then, as I watched and as Zo shook the girl, trying to break her from her trance, the net began moving forward, the tentacles flexing and quivering as it did. As the strings moved, so did the girl, only it wasn't really the girl. It was something inside her that looked just like her.

Something pure.

"We have to stop the net," I said, panicked. "It's pulling her out of her body." I stepped forward and tore at the strings, only to have my hands pass straight through them.

"What net?" Delia and Annabelle asked at the same time.

"You don't see the strings?" I asked, trying desperately to rip them from the girl. The cords moved steadily backward, and the image inside the girl moved farther and farther out of her body. "She's wrapped up in a net of them, and it's . . . it's . . ."

"No!" Zo yelled as the girl's eyes flashed a brilliant blue color.

This shouldn't have been happening. We got there in time, and we should have been able to save her. Whatever this gray stuff was, it was killing her, and there was nothing I could do about it.

The panic spread down my body, and with it, I could feel my blood boiling, the heat surging through my veins.

This wasn't right. It wasn't fair. Something was killing her.

I knew the exact second the heat left my skin. I

wasn't even thinking about the fire or my power, but as I stared at those cords, ripping the girl from her physical form, I hated them. Hated them more than Alexandra Atkins. Hated them more than anything.

The fire leaped from my body to the cords, scorching them with the intensity of my feeling.

"Bailey! You're setting her on fire. Stop it!"

I barely heard Delia's yell. I stared at the cords.

Burn, I thought. Burn.

And just like that, the cords snapped one by one under the force of my flame, and the girl sank back into her body just in time to realize that she was surrounded by fire.

"Aaaahhhhhhh!"

I had to give it to the girl. She knew how to scream.

Delia held her hands out to the fire. "Honey," she yelled.

Instantly, the flames dissolved into honey.

"Aaaahhhhhhh!" The girl continued screaming. Not that I blamed her. For the split second after the scary net of doom had disappeared, she'd been surrounded by flames, and now she was completely covered in honey. Not to mention the fact that the fire and honey had both appeared out of nowhere. I probably would have been freaking out, too.

"Honey?" Zo asked Delia. "Seriously. Honey?"

Delia looked down at her nails. "I don't deal well under pressure," she said.

"Aaaahhhhhhh!"

"Will someone shut her up?" Zo asked, but I could hear the relief in her voice that the girl was still alive enough to be screaming at all. "She's going to blow our cover."

"Stop screaming," Annabelle said gently. "Come inside. Get washed off, and then we'll talk."

"Stop screaming," the girl repeated. Then she looked at us. "Listen, I don't know who you are, but I'm going to go inside and wash this stuff off me. Then, we'll talk."

I stared at Annabelle. The blond girl didn't seem to have any idea that Annabelle had just worked some kind of freaky mind control mojo on her. Until this moment, none of us had realized the full extent of Annabelle's power, or, for that matter, mine.

The second the girl was inside, Zo turned to me. "You set her on fire," she said, awed. "Bay, you wouldn't even set the trash on fire."

"I didn't set her on fire," I said. "I set the tentacles that were pulling her out of her body on fire. There's a difference."

Zo stared at me like I was speaking Indonesian.

"Never mind," I said. "I'll explain when we talk." I glanced back at the spot where the last of the tentacles had been a moment before. Nothing.

"Bay?" Zo's voice broke into my thoughts. "You okay?"

I could feel the heat draining out of my body, and with the heat, every ounce of energy I had. I sat down hard on the ground.

"I'll be okay," I said, barely able to manage a whisper. I sat there for a while, putting all my concentration into breathing.

Apparently, Delia's power wasn't the only one that took a lot out of a person.

As I sat there, I stared out at the ocean. The waves crashed down, and as I watched, the water became a brighter and brighter shade of blue-green that I was all too familiar with. Mist the color of our tattoos rose off the ocean from as far as I could see in any direction, and as I watched, I heard their voices again in my head.

From earth she comes
From air she breathes
From water, her prison beneath the seas

The blue-green color flashed so bright that I had to shield my eyes, and then the rhymes were gone and my head was silent. I wasn't as logical as, say, Annabelle, but I was going to go out on a limb and guess that the ominous "she," whoever she was, had come.

Biting my bottom lip, I grimaced and put my hand to the tattoo on my back.

Safe.

For once, the voice in my head was giving me good news instead of cryptic rhymes or warnings about blood. I breathed a sigh of relief a second too soon.

With the day in majority, the light will block you from her. Do not venture out after nightfall, child. She will find you. She will destroy you and all that you know.

Great, I thought as Adea's voice quieted in my head. World-endy goodness, here we come.

Chapter 8

It was a full hour before the girl we'd saved came out of her hotel bathroom. Apparently, honey wasn't the easiest thing in the world to get out of hair. I had to wonder what Delia's thing was with gooey, nonsolid food substances.

The girl opened her mouth and then closed it again, looking at each of us in turn.

Zo was lying on the couch, completely absorbed in the soccer match that was blaring on the TV. Delia had helped herself to the contents of the fridge and was sipping on a canned mocha. Annabelle was sitting primly in a chair, quietly examining a book lying on the coffee table in front of her.

And me? I was still curled up in a fetal position on the floor. Every now and then, I brought my hand to my tattoo, hoping to hear something useful, but all I got was a whole lot of nothing.

"No offense, but who are you people?" the girl asked.

Delia took a sip of her mocha. "Delia," she said. She was one of those people who liked to believe she could survive on only one name, like Madonna or Cher.

"I'm Bailey," I said, scampering into a sitting position and trying to look less sketchy. "That's Zo."

Zo, her eyes locked on the screen, didn't seem to have any intention of shifting her gaze from the game to the girl standing in front of us. As far as Zo was concerned, we'd saved her, and that was that.

"I don't mean your names," the blond girl said, wrapping her arms around her waist. "I mean what are you doing in my hotel room? And what was up with the fire? And the honey?" She paused, and her eyes narrowed. "Did my mother send you?"

Her mother? What kind of mother did this girl have, anyway?

"You don't really need an explanation," Annabelle said soothingly. "But we'll tell you what we can."

"That's okay," the girl said immediately. "I don't really need an explanation."

Zo grunted, eyes still on the television, a not-so-subtle warning to Annabelle to refrain from ever pulling the mind mojo on the rest of us.

"Why don't you sit down?" Annabelle asked the girl.

"Then we'll talk. You'll have to excuse Zo's manners. She was raised by a group of indigenous swamp wallabies and is at times uncomfortable conversing with civilized humans."

Now that we'd gotten Annabelle talking, she wasn't showing any signs of stopping, and I had to bite my bottom lip to keep from laughing at her completely bizarre insult. It sounded so adult and intelligent and Annabelle.

Zo sat up. A-belle finally had her attention.

The blond girl plopped herself down on the couch, following Annabelle's "request" to a T, and I touched the tattoo on my back, wondering if the big voice people had anything to say about her.

Nothing.

"Look, it's like this—" Zo started to say, but then she interrupted herself. "Swamp wallabies?"

Annabelle arched her eyebrows and stared back at her cousin, her face completely serious. "Your heritage is nothing to be ashamed of, Zo," she said. Without giving Zo a chance to respond, she turned to the girl. "Why don't you tell us your name?"

"I'm Amber," the girl said. Her voice was cute and way peppier than any fifteen(ish)-year-old's voice should have been. With her white-blond hair pulled into a high, wet ponytail, she looked like an Amber.

"And what are you doing here, Amber?" Annabelle asked.

"I'm here with my mom," Amber said, rolling her eyes. "She's here for some retreat thing, and she brought me with her. She thinks it's good for me."

"You didn't want to come," Annabelle said softly. "Because of the circle."

Amber's eyes widened and then she scowled. "Don't tell me you're with *them*," she said. "I can't take any more freaks right now."

"Freaks?" I asked.

"I don't want to talk about it," the girl said.

Delia, Zo, and I looked at Annabelle, waiting for her to convince the girl that she did in fact want to talk about it, but Annabelle remained silent.

"What were you doing out on the balcony?" Zo asked. "Do you remember what happened?"

"I was just watching them . . . the other kids my age here," the girl replied. "And then all of a sudden, you were all there, and I was surrounded by fire and then the fire turned into honey and . . . I'm going insane, aren't I?" The girl paused. "Ohmigod," she said. "You're not even real, are you? I'm hallucinating. I told my mom coming here would traumatize me, and it did."

"We're real," I told her. "Trust me."

The girl looked at me suspiciously, and without another word, she reached out and poked Zo.

"You want to lose that finger?" Zo asked.

The girl shook her head.

"Then don't poke me again."

"Ahem." Annabelle cleared her throat, and Zo

shut her mouth. "Do you remember anything after watching the others?" Annabelle asked softly. "Think back. You were humming, and then you were looking at something."

The girl bit her bottom lip. "I was just thinking about what it would have been like, you know, if things had gone differently." A look came over Amber's face, and I wondered if she was starting to become suspicious of the little mind meld Annabelle was working on her. "I said I didn't want to talk about it."

I thought about the words Annabelle had muttered on the elevator. About the girl having broken a circle; about the others (the people playing volleyball?) being mad at her. About wishing things could be like they were.

So how had she gone from thinking and wishing to being lassoed by a bunch of freaky smoke tentacles?

I met Delia's eyes, and I knew that she was thinking pretty much the same thing, minus the visual of the freaky smoke tentacles.

I leaned forward and sat my chin on my hands, waiting for someone to break the silence.

"Sweet tattoo," Amber said, her eyes on my back. Self-conscious, I pulled my shirt back down over it, only to have it ride back up again. "Is it real?" Amber asked.

"No," I said. "Just temporary." At least, I hoped it was just temporary. At this point, who knew?

"Still pretty sweet," Amber said, filling the silence. "What is it?"

"Not sure," I said. "Some kind of sun, maybe."

"You know," Amber said thoughtfully, "it almost looks like some kind of language or something."

Delia leaned back, showing off her tattoo as well.

"Awesome," Amber said. "You both got one?" She squinted her eyes at Delia's stomach. "Is that one of those Japanese symbols? What does it mean?"

Annabelle practically jumped out of her chair. "Amber, we have to go."

The announcement surprised me, but one look at Annabelle's eyes told me all I needed to know. She knew something the rest of us didn't.

Annabelle hesitated for just a second as she looked at Amber. "You're not crazy," she told her gently. "There really was fire and there really was honey, and you were just a part of something that is a whole lot bigger than us."

Amber nodded. "Bigger than us," she echoed.

"Just remember not to tell anyone," Annabelle said. "And give the circle another shot. The others will forgive you if you ask them to." Annabelle looked at the rest of us. "We should probably get going."

I was suddenly overcome with an incredible urge to get going. Zo was already halfway to the door before she realized what was happening. "Annabelle!"

I giggled at the look on Zo's face.

"You think this is funny?" Zo asked me. "Next thing you know, we'll be alphabetizing our DVDs and—and using little day planners and color-coding things that other people wouldn't even write down."

94

Oh, the horror, I thought, but since I didn't really want a repeat of Zo putting me in a headlock, I kept my mouth shut. As I stepped into the hallway, I glanced back over my shoulder at Amber. Her blond hair was drying quickly, and she still looked more than a little dazed.

"Do me a favor," I said. "Don't hum again for a really, really long time."

Amber gave me a strange look. I didn't blame her. The request didn't make much sense, even to me, but it had just sort of come out of my mouth. I hadn't planned on saying it.

"Okay, sure," Amber said finally. "No humming."

"Goodbye, Amber," Annabelle said.

"Watch yourself," Zo said. "And stay off the balcony."

"Thanks for the mocha," Delia said. "And you might think about layering your hair. I think it would do wonders for your cheekbones."

And with that, we were gone. As soon as the elevator door closed behind us, I turned to Annabelle. "What's going on?" I asked. "Where are we going?"

"And what was she thinking?" Zo asked. "What wasn't she telling us?"

Annabelle was silent for a moment. "That thing she regretted, the circle she kept talking about, I wasn't getting a clear picture, but I think it had something to do with some New Age group she'd joined." She paused. "Her mom's really into that stuff, I guess, something about her heritage. Amber didn't want us to know. She thinks it's freaky."

"Like the floating flames turning into honey isn't?" Delia asked.

Annabelle looked away, carefully avoiding our eyes. "She sort of doesn't think that's all that weird anymore," she said guiltily. "I . . . uh . . ."

"Gotcha," I replied, saving her from having to explain. She really hadn't had much of a choice about the mind control. The last thing we needed was a curious Amber in the middle of all this, whatever all this really was. I could just imagine her popping up, all clueless-like, at the most inopportune time.

The elevator stopped on the fourth floor. When it opened, the same two teenage boys stared back at us. Taking one look at Zo, they made a beeline in the other direction. As soon as the door closed again, the four of us starting cracking up.

"Zo has that effect on boys," Delia said in a mock-serious voice.

Zo elbowed her in the stomach, a grin on her face. "So where are we going again, A-belle?" she asked, changing the subject.

"To the university," Annabelle said plainly, as if it was the most obvious thing in the world.

"As in the place with all the professors and college students?" I didn't quite understand the logic there.

"As in college boys?" Delia asked, a huge grin spreading across her face.

"No," Annabelle said. "More like the university, as in

the place where my mother works, and the place where I know practically the whole linguistics department."

"Linguistics?" I asked. Sometimes Annabelle was a little hard to follow.

Zo caught on first, which I guess made sense. After all, Annabelle *was* her cousin. "You think the tattoos actually mean something?" Zo asked. "That Amber was right and that they are some kind of language?"

"Right now," Annabelle said, "I don't think we have much else to go on."

"It can't hurt," Delia said. "I mean, it's not like we're crunched for time unless Zo gets another one of those oh-my-Gucci-someone-is-dying things."

"Visions," Zo corrected tersely.

I glanced over my shoulder at the ocean as we began to walk toward the bus station. The university was on the other side of town, and my feet were already killing me from walking so much today.

My tattoo throbbed as I watched a wave crash into the shore and remembered what I'd seen earlier. None of my friends had quite known what to make of it, or the thing I'd seen trying to hurt Amber.

I brought my fingers to my tattoo.

Dark. Coming. To find you.

Great, now the voices were speaking in creepy fragments. Like they weren't already hard enough to understand.

"Uh . . . guys?" I said. "There's a slight chance I

might have forgotten to tell you something about that 'all the time in the world' thing." I tore my eyes away from the ocean and looked at my friends. "We sort of can't be out after dark, and it's, like, four-thirty now."

"What?"

"Long story," I told them.

"Bailey." All it took was a single word from Zo, and I spilled my guts.

"You know that freaky green mist stuff and the whole 'she comes' thing that I told you about? Well, whoever's coming, she's coming after dark, and beats me why, but we want to be at home when that happens. . . ."

All three of my friends engaged in some quality synchronized staring in my general direction, so I took a deep breath and started again.

Chapter 9

Four-thirty. T-minus two hours until sundown, and we were taking things one step at a time.

"Hello, Mom."

Annabelle's mother looked at the four of us for a moment before replying. "Hello, Annie." Dr. Porter always confused me. She had A-belle's subtle way of studying people, and she had the same quiet, sensible air, but she also somehow managed to be so incredibly scatterbrained that half the time sensibility never came into the picture.

"Is Lionel around?" Annabelle asked. "I have something I want him to take a look at."

If Annabelle's mother thought it was strange that her fifteen-year-old daughter had something she wanted a professor of ancient languages to look at, she didn't say anything about it. Then again, knowing A-belle, she'd probably grown up asking the adults around her all kinds of obscure academic questions.

"Lionel's in his office," Annabelle's mom said fifteen or twenty seconds later, once she'd remembered we were standing there talking to her. After a beat, she turned to Zo. "Staying out of trouble?" she asked.

"Why, Aunt Sarah, I'm shocked that you would even ask such a question," Zo replied, doing her best Annabelle impression.

Annabelle's mom grinned.

"Mom, don't you have a phone call to make?" Annabelle prompted.

After another conspiratorial wink at Zo, Annabelle's mother disappeared back into her office.

"Tell me you didn't just pull your mind meld mojo on your mom," Zo said.

Delia whistled softly. "I think maybe I got the wrong power," she said. "Mom mind control. Now *that* could take sneaking out to a whole new level."

"I've never snuck out," Annabelle said defensively. "And besides, she really did have an important phone call to make. She'd completely forgotten about it. I just fiddled around in her mind until I found what it was she was forgetting. Nothing"—Annabelle put her hands up to her forehead and made squiggly fingers as I had earlier—"about it."

"In that case," Delia said, "I'll keep my transmogrification, thank you very much. Now, who wants high-lights?"

"Not I," I said immediately.

Delia turned to Zo.

"So help me, Delia, if you bring those evil little fingers of yours anywhere near my hair, you're going to need to transmogrify yourself a body cast. And, hate to break it to you, but given the whole supernatural curfew thing, shouldn't we, you know, be doing something that's not discussing highlights?"

Ignoring the two of them, Annabelle walked down the hallway and knocked on an office door. "Come in," a voice called back. I didn't recognize the accent. Something Slavic, maybe?

Annabelle turned to us. "Can the three of you behave long enough to talk to Lionel?"

"Hey!" I said. "I didn't do anything."

"Says the girl who set Alex on fire yesterday," Delia shot back.

Annabelle put her finger on the doorknob to Lionel's office and gave us each a warning look before she twisted it and opened the door.

"Annie," the accented voice boomed. "You never come to visit an old man anymore."

"I don't know any old men," Annabelle replied, smiling. She paused. "I've brought friends to see you, Lionel."

"You have friends?"

Zo grinned at Lionel's mock-shocked voice as the three of us approached the office. "I think I'm going to like this guy."

"This is Bailey," Annabelle said, setting about making the proper introductions. "The one thoroughly inspecting her nails is Delia, and—"

Zo cut Annabelle off, probably worrying that her introduction was going to include something about being raised by wild monkeys. "I'm Zo," she said sweetly. "Annabelle's cousin."

Zo gave Annabelle a pointed look, and Annabelle rolled her eyes.

"So, why do you visit me today?" Lionel asked from his spot behind a large mahogany desk. He was a big man, with sparkling eyes and a beard too big for his face.

"I have something I'd like you to take a look at, Lionel," Annabelle said. "It's a symbol, perhaps something you might be able to enlighten us on." Now that we were in a university setting, A-belle had switched abruptly into full-on academic mode. To me, she sort of sounded like a robot.

Annabelle crossed over to the desk and picked up a pen. Without being asked, Lionel slid a sheet of paper across the desk to her, and a few quick lines later, Annabelle's crisscrossed crescents were staring back at us from the sheet.

Lionel took the pen from Annabelle and quickly

extended a few of the lines on the paper. "Like this?" he prompted.

Annabelle nodded.

"I've seen this before," Lionel said. "You're right in that. Quite recently, I think. The question is, where?" He pulled on the edge of his beard, twisting it between his thumb and index finger. "Were there other symbols with it?"

Annabelle turned to us, and I could tell from the expression on her face that she couldn't remember exactly what our symbols looked like.

"Annabelle?" Lionel waited.

With a sigh, Annabelle turned around and in one graceful move lifted the hair off the nape of her neck.

Lionel slipped on a pair of green-rimmed glasses and leaned forward. "Why, it's the symbol, Annie," he said. "Where did you get that?"

Annabelle lowered her hair and then looked at me.

Why did I have to go next? Feeling myself on the verge of a blush, I turned around and let my shirt slide up just enough to show the tattoo.

"The others have them, too?" Lionel asked. Annabelle must have nodded, because a second later, he asked me to come closer so that he could get a better look at the symbol on my back. As if this wasn't awkward enough already.

I walked over to his side of the desk and let him take a good look at my back. "Interesting."

I had never thought I'd live to see the day when an eighty-year-old Russian guy thought my back was interesting.

Delia bared her stomach for him as if it was the most natural thing in the world. To the old guy's credit, he didn't so much as blink and merely bent down, getting a good look at the symbol before sketching it and mine onto the notepad next to Annabelle's.

Lionel turned to Zo. "And I suppose you have one as well?" he asked.

Zo opened her mouth and then closed it again. Doing an impressive balancing act, she stood on one foot and pulled the sneaker off the other.

"Your foot?" the older man asked.

"Yes," Zo answered. "You got a problem with that?"

I stared at her. Had the fact that this guy was practically ancient completely escaped her attention? Only Zo would pull the tough-girl routine with an octogenarian.

Lionel chuckled. "This one, she has fire," he told Annabelle. "I like her."

Annabelle couldn't resist the opportunity to give Zo a hard time. "How ironic," she said in a low voice not meant for Lionel's ears. "He thinks *you* have fire."

Absolutely without any ceremony, Zo plopped her foot down on top of Lionel's desk. I'd never realized how freakishly flexible she was.

The fury of lines crissing and crossing each other across her skin, accented with a few thick dots, had Lionel wrinkling his brow.

"What?" we all asked in unison.

"I assume these are all from the same symbol set?" he asked, as if the fact that we were wearing the symbols on our bodies wasn't odd in the least.

"They all came together," I replied.

Lionel looked at Annabelle. "And you think they're all in the same language?" he asked.

Annabelle nodded. "I think so."

Lionel motioned to Zo, and she removed her foot from his desk and sat down in one of the nearby chairs. Lionel gestured for the rest of us to do the same, and then he flew into professor mode, nodding toward the notepad. "These," he said, gesturing to my symbol and Annabelle's, "appear more pictorial in nature." Seeing his words weren't hitting home with anyone but Annabelle, he explained. "They seem to resemble that which they might well represent, like Egyptian hieroglyphics." He gestured between the two symbols. "In this one, we can easily see a sun."

That's what I'd thought it looked like.

"Though the translation could be a myriad of related ideas. Light, fire, day."

"Fire," I said softly. I could practically see the moment when Zo's "why didn't I get a cool power?" answer registered on her face. It hadn't been any big cosmic plan. She'd just picked the wrong tattoo.

"Or it may symbolize something else altogether," Lionel continued. "A lion, for instance."

"What about the other one?" Annabelle prompted, bringing Lionel back from Happy Translation Land.

"If it does go with the first symbol, and I think it might, I'd be tempted to say it was a moon, though of course this is total speculation. The kind that a tenured professor of great standing would never indulge in, you understand."

"Understood," Annabelle said with a nod. "And the others?"

"I can't venture a guess on that one." Lionel brought his pen to touch Delia's tattoo. "However, it's the final symbol that throws me the most. It's smaller than the others, the lines more jagged. Most strikingly, it does not seem to be a pictorial representation of anything. In fact, it looks rather like some mix of Sumerian, Japanese, and early Celtic characters."

"So everyone else has a symbol and I have a letter?" Zo asked. Clearly, she thought she was getting the short end of the tattoo stick yet again.

Lionel shook his head. "There's a continuity among the symbols, if you disregard size. Something about the angles at which the lines intersect or would intersect. The near symmetry, as well, of all the symbols strikes me as odd. These symbols belong together, which makes me question if the first two are indeed hieroglyphic in nature, or if . . ."

Lionel fell into silence, scribbling on the notepad. "If only I could remember where I'd seen the moonlike symbol before," he said.

"In one of these books?" Annabelle asked, gesturing

toward the stacks and stacks of books scattered around the office.

"Perhaps," Lionel said, tugging on his beard. "Perhaps."

The phone rang, and I practically jumped out of my skin. This whole impending doom vibe had me kind of on edge.

"Lionel Kavoslaski." Lionel answered the phone and then put his hand over the mouthpiece. "If you'll excuse me, my dear ones, I have to take this. If you'd like to look through the books, you may."

The four of us huddled in Lionel's doorway to discuss our options.

"That's a whole lot of books," Zo said. "And what's to say there's anything in there about these symbols? What if they aren't even symbols?"

"Do you have a better lead?" Annabelle asked, bristling a bit that Zo was questioning her plan of action. "The lady who sold us the tattoos has disappeared. All we have to go on is Bailey's dreams and these tattoos. You heard what Bay said about this whole 'she comes' business. Even if we hadn't wanted to get to the bottom of this before, I definitely would now."

Translation, I thought: do not argue with the power of my charts.

Zo looked down at her still-bare foot.

"Annabelle's right," I said. "This isn't just about me figuring out a way to not set people on fire anymore.

Something's coming. Something evil. Something big. For all we know, it's already here." This pep talk wasn't turning out the way it had in my mind, but I pushed on. "If these symbols mean something, they might give us a hint about what we're supposed to do to stop it." I paused, looking over at the pile of books, which seemed to have grown about a million times bigger since the last time I had looked.

"What about the voices you hear, Bay?" Delia asked me. I glanced over my shoulder to make sure Lionel wasn't listening, but he was completely absorbed in the phone conversation he was having, which had recently switched over from English to some language I didn't recognize.

I touched my hand to my back.

Dark.

"Just a reminder to be home before dark," I said. "Sheesh. For someone who seems like they might need us to save the world or something, these voice people sure aren't very helpful."

"I can't believe the voices in your head gave us a curfew." Delia blew a strand of chestnut brown hair out of her face. "I mean, honestly, what is the world coming to?"

Somehow, I didn't think we wanted to know the answer to that question.

"What about the names the voice people gave Bailey?" Zo asked finally, still looking for any excuse not to spend what was left of our daylight hours looking through old books that were probably written in languages we couldn't even read. "I mean, if they are real . . . real whatever-they-ares, then shouldn't we be able to find out something about them? And maybe about whatever it is they expect us to fight?"

"Good point," Annabelle said. She sounded almost surprised. "But we all have computers at our houses. We can google there." She paused. "And that's pretty much the only thing we can do after dark, so in the"— A-belle looked at her watch—"one hour and forty-seven minutes of daylight we have left, we'd probably be better off dealing with resources that we don't have at home."

"That would be the books?" Zo asked. Annabelle patted her sympathetically on the shoulder, and Zo sighed.

"It won't be that bad," I consoled Zo, who despised book work about as much as she did water bras and thong underwear.

"Okay," Zo said, playing the martyr to perfection. "I give up. We do the books thing."

"Books," Delia agreed.

"Lead on, Book Girl," I told Annabelle, and with that, the four of us set to work.

One hour, four false leads, two soda runs, and a whole lot of nothing to show for it later, I was starting to question the wisdom of letting Annabelle put us all on book duty. My back was aching, Delia had broken a nail, and Zo looked about half a second away from committing research mutiny.

"That's it," Zo announced. "I'm finished. Done. Completed. *Finito*." She tossed the book she was working on to the floor. Annabelle glared at her and picked the book up, dusting it off all offended-like.

"Maybe she's right, Annabelle," I said. "We've been at this for, like, forever and a half, and we haven't seen anything that looks like any of these symbols."

"I'm thinking of giving myself a tan," Delia mused. "What do you guys think?"

We all glanced at Delia, and then I continued my research-is-evil campaign. "It'll be dark soon," I said, trying to appeal to Annabelle's reasonable side. "We've got a half hour, forty-five minutes tops."

"We won't need it," Annabelle said, a slow smile spreading across her face. Holding open the book Zo had thrown onto the floor, she arched a triumphant eyebrow.

There, on the page, at the bottom, was Annabelle's symbol. Triumphantly Annabelle read the phrase aloud: " 'Thought to be druidic in nature, this lone symbol was recovered at a site in western Ireland at the turn of the century.' "

"Okay, well that does us a whole lot of no good," Zo said. "So somebody who wrote some book thinks that it might be druidic? And what exactly does that tell us? We don't even know what it means."

"Ahhhh, but we will."

The four of us jumped at the sound of Lionel's voice, and Delia, who'd been in the middle of giving herself a homemade tan, turned around, trying not to look suspicious even though she'd only tanned half of her body.

"You think you can translate the symbols?" Zo asked skeptically.

"Now that I know who to call, I might be able to help you," Lionel said. "This book was written a good fifty years ago, my dear. A great deal has been done since then." He looked at his watch. "No good calling just now," he said. "It's getting late, and as it's a Saturday, and as some of my colleagues are a bit less, shall we say, devoted to the trade than I am, perhaps it had best wait until morning."

"We'd better get going," I said, nervous about the whole if-we-stay-out-after-dark-a-nameless-possibly-misty-green-evil-will-smite-us thing.

"You'll call if you learn anything?" Annabelle asked, giving Lionel solemn puppy dog eyes.

"Of course," Lionel said.

"Thanks," Zo said, surprising me.

"Thank *you*, my dears," Lionel returned without so much as pausing. "There are few things I like as much as a good mystery, and these . . ." He gestured to Annabelle's neck and Zo's foot. "These are the things mysteries are made of."

"You're not going to ask why we're wearing the symbols?" Annabelle asked curiously.

Lionel shrugged. "Do I want to know the answer?"

The four of us looked at one another.

"Probably not," I said. He might be a genius with remote ancient languages, but personally, I didn't want to be responsible for giving the guy a heart attack, and the . . . er . . . sensitive nature of the whole tattoos thing could potentially do that to a person. Especially an old person with a large beard.

Annabelle bit back a giggle and lost. "Beard?" she whispered to me the second Lionel turned away. "What does his beard have to do with it?"

We headed for the door. "I liked it better when my thoughts didn't have to be logical," I grumbled. Having Annabelle catch my random thoughts was starting to freak me out. I had a well-developed thought-to-speech filter for a reason.

As we passed through the doorway, I tugged my shirt down over the tattoo, just to make sure.

Dark.

Sheesh. This supernatural curfew thing was getting old fast.

Can't you tell me anything else? I asked silently. Like what exactly this thing is that will come after us if we're out after dark?

The response came from Valgius, his deep, beautiful voice twisted in pain, as if saying these words was burning a hole in his flesh. Slow, unforgiving torture.

She. Is. Sidhe.

Chapter 10

"Hey, Mom?" I called up the stairs. "You up there?"

"Just a minute," she yelled back. I waited. My mom hated it when I just-a-minuted her, but I was used to the inequity of our relationship. She parent, me child. That was just the way these things worked.

Several minutes later, my mom finally deigned to join us. "You girls are back early," she said. "Can I get you something? Cookies? Some dinner?"

Zo opened her mouth, and I could sense a yes coming on. She loved my mom's cooking, and, for that matter, my mom. Through some miracle, given the lightning speed with which Zo typically responded to offers of food, I managed to cut her off before she could accept my mom's invitation. "We're actually eating at Zo's house," I said.

Zo made a face. My mom didn't see it.

"Your dad's turn for the slumber girls?" she asked Zo.

Delia, Zo, and I had been sleeping over at each other's houses practically every Friday and Saturday night for as long as any of us could remember, but we'd outgrown calling them slumber parties when we were like nine, a fact that had obviously escaped my mother's attention.

"I'm just going to go grab my stuff," I said. "I wanted to make sure it was okay."

As on top of me as my parents could be about everything else, they almost never said no to a weekend sleepover across the street, especially given the fact that my mom had gotten to play hostess the night before.

"No problemo," my mom said. "Do you girls at least want to eat dinner over here first? I could throw together a lasagna. Or some chicken curry. Or—"

"We already promised we'd eat at Zo's," I said, cutting her off. I was notoriously bad at keeping secrets from my mom and thus wanted to keep our time together at a minimum until this whole thing blew over. As it was, it was all I could do not to blurt out everything. I was half afraid that if she asked me one more time if she could fix us anything, I'd blurt out, "Yes, could you fix us something that will get rid of ancient evils?" to which my mom would inevitably reply, "Wouldn't you rather have a nice roast?" before realizing what I'd just said.

I shuddered at the very idea of it.

"Come on," I said, practically dragging Zo and Annabelle up the stairs. Delia had gone across the street to her house to pick up a few "extra necessities" and was supposed to meet us over at Zo's house in five minutes.

"Remind me again why exactly it is that we have to spend tonight at my house?" Zo asked as soon as my bedroom door was closed behind us. "My dad's a terrible cook."

Annabelle guiltily nodded her agreement.

"You'll live," I said. "We'll order pizza or something." I grabbed the overnight bag I always kept packed and threw in an extra pair of underwear. "And we have to spend the night at your house, because my mom and dad are way too with it for their own good, or ours. We're going to be researching this thing, and I can't get within a five-foot radius of my mom without her little mom radar clicking on."

My mom had a history of knowing everything I did before I did it. Her accuracy was downright freaky.

"She'd totally go all Annabelle on us and pull all that juicy info right out of our heads," I said as I zipped my bag shut.

"I think I may resent that comment," Annabelle said thoughtfully. "Not sure."

"Let's just get out of here before the radar goes off."

"Did it ever occur to you, Bay, that it may not be that your mom's freakishly perceptive? You may just be a really, really bad liar." Zo pointed out the obvious.

"A little bit of column A, little bit of column B," I

replied. "Now can we just get out of here?" Without a word, Annabelle and Zo grabbed their stuff and Delia's from the night before, and we trooped down the steps.

We were halfway out the front door when my mom stopped us. "What did you say the fabulous foursome is up to tonight?" she asked us.

I looked from Annabelle back to Zo. "Nothing much," I said. "We'll probably order some pizza, go online . . ."

She didn't seem to be buying it, and I hadn't even lied yet.

Quick, I thought, distract her with talk of the dance. My mom was always up for some quality high school discussion, especially if she thought there was even a chance that it might involve boys.

". . . talk about the dance, that kind of thing," I finished up.

She took the bait. "Oh, the dance on Monday," she said. "I'd almost forgotten. Anyone going with a date?"

Success.

"Mom, we gotta go," I said. "Delia's meeting us over there, and if she gets there before we do, she'll probably redo Zo's entire wardrobe or something."

Zo's eyes lost all glint of the humor they'd shown at my mom's not-so-subtle boy talk. For all we knew, Delia was already over there transforming Zo's worn-out boys' sweatshirts into tube tops.

My mom took one look at Zo's stricken face and

laughed out loud. Thirty seconds and two promises to call if we needed anything later, we were out the door.

"I swear, if she touches any of my stuff with those change-happy fingers of hers . . ." Zo cut off as Delia came out of her front door and met us on the sidewalk in front of Zo's house.

"Miss me?" she asked teasingly.

"But of course," I replied. "Now, let's get re-searchy."

Zo and her dad lived alone in the house across the street from mine and had since the big mom fiasco eleven years before. Luckily, her dad usually went to his favorite sports bar on Saturday nights, so we didn't have to worry about adult interference for a while.

Zo, thinking of food (big surprise there), made a beeline for the phone as soon as she got into the house, and the rest of us made a beeline for Zo's dad's study. More specifically, we made a beeline for Zo's dad's computer.

Annabelle sat down at the keyboard, and before I could so much as blink, she pulled up a search engine. "How do you spell Adea?" she asked.

"Don't search for that first," I surprised myself by saying. "Search for Sídhe." Without being asked, I spelled it out for her. "S-Í-D-H-E."

"Whatever you say," Annabelle said. I'd told them what Valgius had gone to great pains (from the sounds of it, literally) to tell me about our cryptic and currently vague enemy, but I don't think the enormity of it had hit them the way it had hit me.

In my dream, Valgius had said he was Sídhe like it was the first thing on his list of defining characteristics. Like if I was making a list, and female and good friend and decent student and horrible dancer were all on there, all of that would have been below whatever was as important to me as being Sídhe was to Valgius. Then, boom, he'd told me that whoever this nameless evil being was, she was Sídhe, too.

It killed him to say it, even discounting the difficulty he'd had making me hear it.

Annabelle's hands flew across the keys, and she'd made it through several links by the time Zo walked into the study.

"Pizza will be here in no time," she said. "One cheese and one supreme with extra pepperoni."

One guess as to which one Zo was planning on eating.

"You guys find anything interesting?"

"We're looking up Sídhe," I said. "Since that's what Valgius and Adea are, and since that's what Val said this bad thing was, I thought it would be a good place to start."

"Val?" Zo asked, raising an eyebrow at me. "As in Valgius?"

"We both know I'm totally too lazy for three syllables," I said, and a private look passed between the two of us. There was a reason Zo was Zo and not Zoe-Claire (other than the obvious what-were-her-parents-thinking thing), and I was that reason. Was it any wonder I'd earned her eternal loyalty?

"Here we go," Annabelle said finally, interrupting my trip down memory lane. " 'Sídhe: in Celtic mythology, a royal race of fairies, led by—' "

"Wait a second," Zo said. "Just back up the babbling wagon, there. Fairies? Royal? Royal fairies? Are you trying to tell me that this awful, world-ending, us-destroying thing we were given these powers to stop is some kind of royal *fairy*?"

I thought about the way Valgius had referred to the it as a she. It was hard to think of it as a person. Or a Sídhe. Or whatever.

"A fairy princess," I said out loud, and I could completely understand the incredulous expression on Zo's face. All this doom-and-gloom, world-at-stake hoopla over a *fairy princess*? Something about that seemed wrong on so many levels.

"It might not be a fairy princess," Delia put in thoughtfully. "It could be a fairy duchess, or a fairy countess, or a fairy viscountess . . ."

For a brief time in seventh grade, Delia had been obsessed with British royalty in all its forms.

". . . or a fairy lady or a fairy dowager duchess, or a fairy dowager countess . . ."

"It says here," Annabelle said, as Delia prattled on about all the glorious royal fairy possibilities, "that the Sídhe were thought by some to be a race of warriors."

Annabelle's hands flew over the keys, and she hit another link with the mouse. "This one says that 'sídhe' with a lower-case 's' refers to a hill, or a fairy mound."

"More fairies," Zo grumbled.

"These fairy mounds were thought to be passages to the Otherworld, especially at certain times of the year. It was at these times, such as Samhain on October thirty-first, that the Tuatha de Danaan were thought to pass from the Otherworld into our realm."

"The whosit de what?" I asked.

"Tuatha de Danaan," Annabelle replied, wrinkling her forehead as she read on. "Another name for the Sídhe, I think. It means 'Children of Dana.'" Annabelle paused and read on. "Some kind of ancient earth goddess or something to that effect."

"Bad flashbacks of seventh grade and Greek mythology," Zo said. "Did I mention how much I hated our unit on Greek mythology? Because I did."

Delia poked Zo in the side with a playful grin. "You only hated it because we spent most of our time on Aphrodite and the Muses and they were too girly for your tastes," she said.

"No," Zo said. "I hated it because the other section got to do a unit on samurais, and we were stuck talking about who gave fire to who and who was kidnapped to the underworld by who." Zo wrinkled her nose. "I swear, Greek mythology is the ancient equivalent of a giant cosmic soap opera. I kept waiting for Aphrodite's twin sister to come back and push her down a well in order to try to take over her life."

"Somebody's been watching soap operas," Delia said in a singsong voice.

"Have not," Zo said, a little too quickly. Delia kept on grinning like a Cheshire cat.

"Guys . . ."

I turned to look at Annabelle. Her eyes flitted back to the screen.

"What?" the rest of us asked at once.

"The Sídhe were known for their spell-casting ability."

We stared blankly back at her.

"Those words you heard when we applied the tattoos, Bailey," Annabelle reminded me. "Do you think it might have been a spell?"

"Sure," I said. "It makes sense." A horrible thought occurred to me. "If Adea and Valgius are Sídhe, and they can cast a spell that gives us these powers, then what exactly can this third evil Sídhe do?"

"I don't know about you guys," Zo said, "but I have a little trouble being intimidated by a fairy princess. What's the worst she can do?"

Delia's mouth dropped open, and she smacked Zo. "Haven't you ever seen a horror movie?" she demanded, hands on her hips. "That's exactly the type of thing people say right before something horrible happens."

For a moment, the three of us sat there in silence.

Ding. Dong.

"Aaaaahhhhhhh!" I yelped despite myself.

Zo, Annabelle, and Delia broke into a fit of giggles. "Doorbell," Annabelle said mildly, her eyes still laughing.

"Right," I said. "Doorbell."

Zo jumped up and sauntered out of the room. I followed her.

"This is where the axe murderer comes in," Delia said, on my heels.

I turned around and glared at her.

"What?" she said. "You've seen as many horror movies as I have. I speak the truth."

Zo ignored both of us and flung open the front door.

The pizza delivery boy stared at us humorlessly. I didn't exactly blame him. Chances were, if I was a pizza boy, I wouldn't be too chipper, either.

"That'll be sixteen seventy-five," he said in a bored voice.

Zo turned to me. "The money's on the counter," she said. "Can you grab it?"

I didn't have to ask to know that while I was getting the money, Zo would be inspecting the pizza. There were few things in life that Zo took more seriously than pizza.

I'd been in Zo's house so often that I could have walked the path from the front door into the kitchen blindfolded. I knew exactly where her father usually left money for food.

"Not here," I yelled back.

"Try in the first drawer," Zo yelled back. "Maybe it fell in or something. Look under the blue notepad."

I opened the drawer and picked up the blue note-pad, ignoring the makeshift shopping list Zo's dad had put together, and grabbed the twenty that sat underneath it. By the time I got back to the front door, Zo had eaten half a slice of pizza, and Delia and the pizza boy were laughing and staring holes into each other.

I handed him the money. "Thanks," he said, never taking his eyes off Delia. Or, more precisely, never taking his eyes off Delia's chest.

"Guys?" Annabelle's voice rang down the stairs. "You need to come check this out."

"Pizza," Zo yelled back up the stairs.

"This is important, Zo," Annabelle yelled back. For someone as quiet as she was, A-belle had a heck of a set of lungs on her.

"More important than pizza?"

"Yes."

Zo sighed. "Come on," she said. "The practical one calls."

Delia batted her eyelashes at the pizza boy one last time. I wasn't really sure why she bothered with the eyelashes. He was so entranced with her breasts that I doubted he could even see her eyes.

"Maybe I'll see you around," Delia said.

The pizza boy gazed adoringly at her. "Sure," he said, a huge grin on his face.

"Bye," Delia said.

"Sure," the boy repeated, his eyes still locked on her chest.

Delia giggled and gave us a helpless grin as Annabelle told us to hurry again. After another five seconds of the pizza boy not getting the hint, Zo took matters into her own hands.

"Allow me to demonstrate something," she said. She pointed to Delia's face. "This is Delia's face." Zo's hands moved downward. "And I can see you're already acquainted with her breasts. Believe it or not, her face just said goodbye, so I'm afraid you and her breasts are going to have to cut this little moment short."

Without saying another word, Zo closed the door on him. She grabbed another slice of pizza and headed up the stairs.

"Zo!" Delia shrieked.

Zo didn't even turn around. "You can thank me later."

Delia huffed, but I knew for a fact she didn't mind it. If it wasn't for Zo, Delia would have spent her entire life trying to get guys to look at her face. I wondered if the boy was still standing on the front porch, staring at the spot where Delia's chest had been a moment before. I wouldn't have been surprised.

"So, what's the four-one-one?" I asked Annabelle as soon as the three of us had made it into the study.

Annabelle opened her mouth to answer, but Zo pre-empted her.

"I come bearing pizza," Zo said solemnly, handing her cousin a piece as the four of us crowded around the computer screen.

Annabelle accepted the pizza gracefully, and, satisfied with her research prowess, began to nibble on it as the rest of us took in the information she'd dug up.

" 'Daughters of Adea,' " I read out loud. It took about three seconds after I'd read the words for me to figure out what I'd said. "Daughters of Adea?"

"It's a New Age group," Annabelle said. "I googled Adea, and this is what I got. That *is* how you spell it, isn't it, Bailey?"

I nodded. "I think so," I said.

"That's it?" Zo asked between bites of pizza. I had a feeling that in the battle of pizza versus Annabelle's breakthrough, the pizza was on the verge of winning more of Zo's attention.

"I haven't gotten to the best part," Annabelle said. She scrolled down the page.

There, staring back at us, was a very familiar symbol: two overlapping crescents. Without a word, Annabelle lifted the hair off her neck. "They're nearly identical," she said, rubbing her thumb gently over her tattoo.

"Okay, now we're talking near-pizza-level impressive here." High praise from Zo.

"Wow," Delia said, her eyes lighting on something else on the page. "Way impressive."

"What?" I asked. A moment later, my eyes found what Delia had seen.

"A retreat?" I asked.

"Not just any retreat," Annabelle said. She clicked on the link and a new page was opened. "A retreat held in celebration of Mabon." She paused for a moment. "At the Richmond Hotel."

My eyes widened. "Amber," I said. "She was there with her mom for some retreat, and remember, Annabelle picked up on all of those New Age vibes."

"Are you telling me we spent all that time at the university, and the answer was at the Richmond all along?" Zo asked.

We were silent. Somehow, I had a feeling I knew what we were going to be doing the next day.

A pale green light filled the air from behind me, and I turned around.

"You so did not just transmogrify pizza into a salad," Zo said, absolutely horrified. "That's like sacrilege."

"House salad with balsamic vinaigrette," Delia confirmed.

"That is just wrong on so many levels," Zo said, holding her piece of pizza closer to her, protecting it from Delia's transmogrifying fingertips.

Annabelle giggled at the look of pure horror on her cousin's face, and then, to cover it up, she raised her pizza slice in the air. "To tomorrow," she said, and then we toasted: my half-eaten crust clinking with Zo's

126

fourth piece of pizza and Delia's newly transmogrified salad fork.

To Adea, I thought, wondering what secrets the next day would bring.

"To pizza," Zo said, sneaking a bite from a piece that seemed to have just appeared in her other hand.

"To us," Delia corrected. "For being so utterly fabulous."

Even Zo had to grin.

"To us."

Chapter 11

Come, come, to fight, to live, she comes.

I opened my eyes to the sound of water falling on stone. I turned over and ran my hands over the stone seal beneath me, feeling its crevices. Even staring directly at it, I was overwhelmed with the sense that I wasn't really seeing; that I couldn't see it.

"You see more than you think you do."

"Adea." Her name escaped my throat before I even knew I'd opened my mouth.

"There's power in a name," she said. "Power to the one who says it."

I stared at her, trying to comprehend. "Trust me," I said. "I don't have any power."

Except for that whole pesky fire thing, I thought.

"You have more than you think," she said.

"In the blood."

I whirled around to see Valgius standing behind me, his hair glowing a true black underneath its soft but brilliant blue sheen. "The power is in the blood," he said.

A green mark, so dark it was almost black, slashed across his forehead, marking the otherwise perfect tawny skin. Without thinking, I reached up to touch it.

"You're hurt," I said.

His eyes stared over my head at Adea.

"Aye, child," she said. "He's hurt."

"It's nothing," he said, every inch the warrior Annabelle had said the Sidhe were thought to be.

"We know war," Adea said sadly, lifting the thought from my mind, "but we aren't meant for it. Not anymore." For a moment, her eyes glazed over with memories, but she shook her head slightly, her ruby black hair shaking as she did. "She's free now, and the balance grows weaker. We grow weaker." She touched my shoulder softly. "She cannot know you're here, cannot know that you've seen the Seal."

"She knows humans," Valgius said. "That was her choice, to live among you, to steal your power so that she might destroy us."

"You are her playthings," Adea spit out, anger clear in the lines of her face.

Valgius's voice stayed calm. "She knows humans, and do not be fooled, daughter, she knows you."

Me? She knew me?

"She doesn't know what you've seen. She doesn't know the powers you bear, but she knows you."

Adea caught my chin in her hands. Soft hands, cool to the touch like the stone itself.

"She knows you. Never forget that."

I could feel a sob rising in my throat, and I wasn't sure why. "What do you want from me?" I asked. "What do you expect me to do? I don't even know what she's trying to do, let alone how to stop it. I don't even know who she is." Tears ran down my cheeks. "Who is she?"

With gentle hands, Adea wiped the tears from my face.

"I don't even know her name," I whimpered. "You said names have power. How can I stop her if I don't even know her name?"

The tears she'd wiped from my face clung to her fingertips. Reverently, Adea brought her lips to her hands and blew my tears off her fingers. They fell, like raindrops out of the sky, onto the stone we were standing on; onto the Seal.

Instantly, a wave of power shot through the room, extending out in a circle from the Seal.

"May your tears keep us safe," Adea whispered.

"Safe from what?" I asked.

"Alecca."

"Alecca." I woke with the name on my lips and groped around in the dark for something to write with. I couldn't forget the name. Names were power.

"Alecca," I said under my breath. "Alecca."

"With those shoes?" a sleeping Delia murmured incredulously. "You have *got* to be kidding me."

"Alecca," I whispered the name again, and when I finally found a pen, I breathed a sigh of relief.

With each letter, I said the name aloud. "Alecca. Alecca. Alecca."

It didn't sound particularly evil. Honestly, it sounded kind of like a fairy princess name.

I looked down at the paper, and as I stared at the name, I felt a chill spread up my body. My limbs went cold, and I found myself absolutely unable to move.

She knows you.

I shook the memory of Adea's words from my mind and forced myself to move. Slowly, the heat came back into my body. My left arm throbbed, and I looked down. Even in the dark, I could see the cut, shallow and thin, spread across my skin.

"The Blood of the Sídhe." I whispered the words before I realized what I was doing.

"Bailey?"

I turned to look at Zo. Her blond hair was a mess from her sleeping bag. "You okay, Bay?"

I glanced down at my arm. The cut was gone.

"Bay?"

"I'm okay," I said softly, careful not to wake the others.

Zo crawled over her sleeping bag toward me and then, without a word, she threw her arms around my shoulders.

"You know I've got your back," she said. "You know that, right, Bay? No matter what. It's you and me."

"I know," I said, and all of a sudden, I was in kindergarten again, and Zo, blond pigtails waggling in fury, was demanding to know who'd made me cry so that she could make them eat dirt. Literally.

"Pleats?" Delia whimpered in her sleep. "No pleats."

Zo's expression never faltered. "I'm not gonna let anything hurt her, either, Bay," she said. "Or Annabelle."

Zo, in her pajamas, was ready to take on the world for us, armed with nothing but premonitions and what every teacher she'd ever had had defined as an "attitude problem."

I loved her for it.

"You look tired," Zo said. "Go back to sleep." From the tone of her voice, I inferred that I'd been given my orders. Obediently, I lay back down, and I was nearly asleep when I noticed that Zo was still sitting up, and her eyes were open. She was watching me. Guarding me. Guarding all of us.

I closed my eyes again and hoped that Zo would soon do the same.

"You're beautiful."

"No," I said, staring back into his eyes. "You are."

He laughed then. "You surprise me," he said. "Everything about you surprises me."

I could feel his breath on my face, and it made my skin heat up.

"*Your eyes surprise me every time I look into them and they're looking back at me.*" He brought his hands gently to the side of my face. "*Your mouth surprises me, because you always seem to smile more with one half than with the other, like part of you knows a funny secret that none of the rest of us, not even your other half, can guess.*"

He brushed a finger over my lips, and I sucked in a breath. This was so right. It all felt so right.

"*You surprise me, Bailey Morgan,*" he said. We swayed to the music, and the tune filled my head. This was so right, and I wanted it with all of my being. Wanted him.

"*Kane,*" I said. There was so much to ask him. He could have any girl. Why me? He hadn't even really known my name, and now I was surprising him?

"*Just dance with me,*" he whispered back. "*That's all I want, Bailey.*" He paused. "*You. Me. Right now.*"

We continued dancing, moving as one to the strange music that coursed through our bodies and into the air. His hand moved from my face and down my arm. I winced.

"*You're hurt,*" he said tenderly.

I looked down at the red scratch on my left arm. Where had that come from? I couldn't remember.

Without another word, he brought his lips to my arm, and silently pressed them to the cut. "*There,*" he said, "*all better.*"

And when he said it, everything *was all better*. There was nothing to worry about. There was just me, and Kane, and our dance.

He brought his lips close to mine. "All better," he said again. "Just the way it should be."

"The way it should be," I repeated, and my lips gravitated toward his.

And then, he was gone.

"You wake me up at the crack of dawn, but you won't even let me throw a pillow at her?"

"She might be dreaming something important." I recognized Annabelle's patented "I am sensible, hear me roar" voice.

"I was dreaming about Juicy Couture," the first voice replied. "And you don't think that's important?"

Groaning slightly, I rolled over onto my side and opened my eyes.

"Morning, sunshine," Zo said.

"Good afternoon's more like it," Delia grumbled. "Did you know that they got me up at seven, Bailey? Seven!" Delia was clearly scandalized that there were people in this world who got up at seven o'clock, let alone that one of them would have had the audacity to wake her up at that ungodly hour.

"We wanted to maximize our use of daylight hours," Annabelle explained to me. After a full night's sleep, she seemed more in academic mystery-solving mode than ever.

Zo cleared her throat.

"Fine," Annabelle admitted. "*I* wanted to maximize our use of daylight hours, and Zo wanted to go for a run and then eat what, as best I can tell, was the majority of a very large pig."

"So you woke me up why?" Delia asked, not letting go of it.

"Because you take five times as long to get ready as anyone else, and we wanted to be ready to go when Bailey woke up," Zo said, answering for Annabelle without any psychic prompting.

"What time is it?" I asked.

"A little after noon," Delia said. "I've been ready for three hours, and I couldn't exactly go back to sleep after I got dressed."

I got up from my sleeping bag and gave Delia a small hug. "Would it make you feel better if I let you give me highlights?" I asked.

Delia's eyes lit up. "Maybe," she said. "Can I give you colored contacts, too?"

"I don't wear contacts," I said.

Delia rolled her eyes. "You know what I mean," she said. "Well, can I?"

I sighed, but thinking of Delia up at the crack of dawn, and poor Annabelle and Zo listening to her complain while they all waited for me to wake up from another Kane dream, I had to give in.

"Fine," I said, "but we put it all back like it used to be before my mom sees me."

"Agreed," Delia said. "You get dressed, and I'll warm up."

I didn't ask how exactly she was going to warm up to

changing the color of my eyes. I was pretty sure I didn't want to know. Moving quickly, I slipped on a pair of jeans and a white T-shirt.

"Okay," I said, feeling as if I was about to face a firing squad. "Just get it over with."

Delia looked at me and then nodded. "Honey blond and amber streaks," she said, running her hands over my hair.

"Amber," I remembered, the second Delia said the word. "The retreat."

Delia snapped her fingers to get my attention. "Eyes first," she said. "Now don't blink, or you're going to end up with really weird-looking eyelids."

"You know," Zo mused, "that could come in handy. You're in class, and you're sleeping, only your eyelids look just like your eyes, so . . ."

Annabelle shook her head. "Only you," she said to Zo.

Zo grinned.

My eyes were starting to sting from holding them open for so long.

"Done," Delia said. She turned me toward the wall, and with another wave of her hand turned Zo's soccer poster into a full-sized mirror.

"You didn't . . . now, that's just wrong, you can't . . . soccer . . . mirror . . ."

I barely even heard Zo's words. There had to be some trick to this poster-mirror. I was pretty sure that

that couldn't have been me in the reflection. The high-lights brought out the blond tone in my hair, but at the same time, made the brown parts look darker, more dramatic. My skin practically glowed next to my new hair color, and then I looked into my own eyes.

They were blue. Shockingly, unapologetically blue.

Delia examined her work. "A little more dramatic than what I had pictured," she said, "but all in all, I think it's stunning."

I couldn't tear my eyes away from my reflection. My hair shined as it had never shined before, the colors blending together to make me look . . . almost . . .

"Pretty." Annabelle lifted the word from my mind.

I looked at Delia. "I love it," I said, "but the eyes might be a little much."

"I'll trade you the eyes for a different shirt," Delia said.

"What's wrong with my shirt?"

"Don't make me go there," Delia said.

"I thought this whole transmogrification thing was supposed to make her really tired," Zo said, still in shock over the loss of her soccer poster.

Delia grinned. "I think this power is growing on me," she explained. "Or I'm growing on it." She lifted her hands to my face and imperiously commanded my eyes to return to their normal color. Then, before I knew what was happening, she turned an appraising look on my shirt. She held her hand over it and whispered

137

something I couldn't quite hear. Almost immediately, my shirt began melding itself into something else, right there on my body.

"Delia!" I yelped. "This isn't a shirt. This is like two-thirds of a shirt, max."

Zo, who'd finally managed to stop looking where her poster used to be, clapped me on the shoulder. "Take one for the team, Bay."

I gaped at her. Zo Porter, queen of the boyish sweat-shirt, was telling me to wear this low-cut, belly-showing, almost see-through number to "take one for the team"?

Annabelle giggled and then cleared her throat. "We should be going," she said. "We're already down to barely seven hours of daylight, and we don't know how things are going to go at the retreat."

I was supposed to go out in public looking like this?

"So what did you dream last night?" Annabelle asked me curiously.

I opened my mouth, but all I could think about was the fact that I felt more or less topless.

"It's a statement," Delia told me encouragingly. "And you look fabulous." She wiggled her eyebrows at me. "Let's hope we run into Kane again."

"Bailey." Annabelle tried to get me back on topic. "Did you dream?"

I nodded.

Annabelle nodded back at me. "Can you tell us about it on the way to the Richmond?"

I immediately started for the door. "Come on, guys," I said, ready and roaring to get this day under way. "I'll tell you about my dream on the way to the Richmond."

Silence fell over the room for about two full seconds, and then, at the exact same moment, Zo and I realized what had just happened.

"Annabelle!"

Even I had to laugh at the guilty expression on her face, and then, we were on our way for real—me, my "shirt," my new highlights, and all.

Chapter 12

"Okay," Zo said as we stepped into the hotel lobby. I could tell by her tone of voice that she was practically rubbing her hands together at the thought of interrogating some fairy worshippers, good cop/bad cop–style. "Who's first?"

"People skills," Annabelle reminded her cousin. "This is going to take people skills."

"I have people skills," Zo insisted.

The rest of us remained suspiciously quiet.

"We need to be covert." Annabelle tried a slightly different approach. "And . . ." She trailed off as Delia approached a woman to our left.

"What can you tell me about Adea and the Sídhe?" Delia demanded. The woman stared at her. Delia spoke again, more slowly this time. "What. Can. You." Delia gestured toward the woman to clarify that last word. "Tell. Me." Another clarifying gesture. "About—"

Annabelle snatched Delia's arm and pulled her aside. "You call that covert?"

"I'd be glad to tell you about Adea," the woman said.

Delia arched an eyebrow triumphantly at Annabelle.

"Adea is a state of mind," the woman said. She smiled serenely. "Adea is a philosophy of the heart. Adea is water and earth. Adea is fire and air."

I felt like raising my hand and mentioning the fact that I had personally met Adea, and that she hadn't been particularly watery, or airy, or . . .

"But the actual personage of Adea," Annabelle pressed. "Are there stories surrounding her existence?"

"You misunderstand," the woman said. "Adea is not a person."

"She's Sídhe," I murmured.

The woman looked at me strangely out of the corner of her eye. I shut my mouth.

"Adea," the woman said. "A Dawn Ever Always."

"A Dawn Ever Always?" we all repeated.

"The Daughters of Adea believe that a new light is always around the corner," the woman said. "That there is light in nature, and that we must take our place in the light, give ourselves to—"

"Invigorating," Zo said. "Excuse us for just one second."

There was no doubt about it. She was a charmer.

"Okay, so how did we miss out on the fact that Adea was an acronym?" Zo voiced the question on everyone's mind.

"A Dawn Ever Always," Annabelle said incredulously. "That's not even grammatical."

"Call it a guess," Zo said, "but I'm going to go out on a limb here and bet that no one in this entire place has even heard of the Sídhe, let alone knows anything about the Adea that could actually help us."

"You'd be wrong."

I jumped about three feet in the air at the sound of a voice that most definitely wasn't one of the four of us.

"I don't mean to frighten you."

And that, of course, made it all better. I turned around, unsure what exactly to expect.

The woman greeted me with a smile. "I couldn't help but overhear," she said. "You're looking for information on Adea." She lowered her voice. "And on the others."

"The others?"

"Come," the woman said. "We'll be more comfortable in my room. We can speak more openly there."

My friends and I glanced at one another. The woman's creepy-serene tone was like something out of a movie, and I couldn't help but think that in the movie, the woman's character would probably be planning on killing our characters and eating us for supper.

"All right," Annabelle said after a few seconds.

I swallowed hard and then wondered what I was

afraid of. There were four of us, and one of her, and I was going to go with my gut and guess that she probably couldn't set things on fire. Plus, Zo's premonitions had to have been good for something other than the occasional Amber saving. If this woman had been, for instance, planning our impending doom, wouldn't some light in Zo's head have gone off?

I swallowed again when we reached our destination and the woman opened the door to her room. I touched my hand to my tattoo as I stepped in. No words of advice came into my mind. That was a good sign, right?

"Bailey," the woman said as the door closed behind her. "You worry too much."

"How did you know her name?" Zo asked, her voice low and steely. When she got into protective mother-bear mode, it could get really ugly really quickly, but the woman's smiling expression didn't change. "The same way I know that your name is Zo," the woman said, "and that the one examining the earrings on the coffee table is Delia."

"She knows the same way I know." Annabelle's voice was even, her tone appraising.

"Mind reader." Zo's words came out like an accusation.

"Unintentional, I assure you," the woman said. "I am Keiri."

"Annabelle," Annabelle said. After a split second, she paused. "How is that I knew your name and you didn't know mine?" she asked.

143

Keiri shrugged. "You're blocked," she said. "Fairy magic, I believe."

"Forgive me for not speaking fluent freaky," Zo snapped, "but what's that supposed to mean?"

"Is that the question you really want answered?" Keiri asked.

"No," I said slowly, a million better questions racing through my mind. Fairy? As in Sídhe? What did all this have to do with my very close personal friends, the big voice people?

"Coffee?"

"Sure," Delia replied immediately. "I like the earrings, by the way," she said. "They're a nice color."

"They're soothing," Keiri said, moving to pour the coffee for us as we sat. Tentatively, I took one of the earrings in my hand. The purple stones were small, perfectly symmetrical teardrops.

"Amethyst," Keiri said. "It calms excess energy."

"Uh-huh." Zo, always the skeptic, leaned back in her chair. "Likely story."

Keiri, not at all put off by Zo's skepticism, handed me a cup of coffee. "Things of beauty can have secondary purposes," she said. "I'd think you four would know that by now."

So she knew about the tattoos. Rubbing my thumb over the rim of my coffee cup, I wondered how it was that she knew about our powers but hadn't picked up on my intense dislike of coffee.

"Can you tell us about Adea?" I blurted out, half afraid that she'd pick the anti-coffee thought right out of my head and take offense.

"And not the 'A Dawn Whatever Whatever' one," Zo ordered, still playing the tough guy.

Keiri clicked her tongue behind her teeth and shook her head. "They mean well," she said. "The Daughters. I found the group online. Imagine my surprise when I joined and found that no one knew of Adea, that none came from Guardian lines."

"Guardian lines?" I asked.

"Let me tell you what I know," Keiri said, "and then you can ask whatever questions you like." She paused. "My parents died when I was nine. My brother and sister went to live with our uncle, but I went to our grandmother."

I brought the cup of coffee to my lips just to keep from asking what any of this had to do with Adea. I took a tiny sip and felt my gag reflex lurch as the coffee hit my tongue. It tasted (not surprisingly) like coffee. I hated coffee.

"Long story short," Keiri said, looking at me with an almost-grin, "my grandmother was what most people would call an eccentric." She took a sip of her own coffee. "She didn't get out of her house much, didn't speak to many people."

"She saw the future," Annabelle said softly. "And the past."

Keiri nodded. "She was a dream seer. Her dreams often came true, and she often dreamed of the past. She'd learned early on to distrust others."

And the irrelevant information just keeps coming, I thought.

"Don't be so impatient," Keiri told me. "It's the past that she dreamed about that concerns you." She took another long drink of coffee. "Tell me what you know."

"Can't *you* tell us what we know?" Zo asked. "You seem to be good at that."

Annabelle shot Zo a long, warning look, and then turned back to Keiri. "We know that we've been given these powers for a reason." Annabelle lifted one eyebrow in question. "I assume you know about our powers?"

Keiri inclined her head slightly.

"Adea and Valgius, they've been appearing to Bailey since the first night. She hears their voices. We know that there's some kind of evil Sídhe out there, and she's got some kind of grudge against the others. We know that Adea and Valgius want us to stop her. We know that it's dangerous for us to be out after dark."

"We know that her name is Alecca," I said. Just saying the name made me nervous. "She's getting stronger, and the others are getting weaker. I think she wants to kill Adea and Valgius and . . . ummm . . . maybe, you know, get rid of us in the process."

After I spoke, there was a long silence.

146

Way to be a downer, Bailey, I thought.

After a few seconds, Delia picked up the slack. "We know that all three of them—Adea, Val, and this other chick—are Sídhe, and that Sídhe are some kind of royal fairy warrior witches."

Keiri arched an eyebrow at the description. "That is all?" she asked.

Were we supposed to know more? I thought we'd done pretty decently for being new to the whole World of Freaky scene.

"To begin with, rid your mind of your ideas of fairies. The Sídhe aren't, and have never been, the creatures you imagine them to be. They're human enough in appearance, but magical energy that no mortal mind can truly comprehend runs through their blood. Imagine the ocean during a storm: waves crashing, wind beating down against the water, lightning ripping through the air. That's the kind of power that flows through Sídhe veins.

"Theirs is a power of life. Their life. Our lives."

Keiri looked at each of us in turn. "And it is with our lives, human life, that our story truly begins, because Sídhe power feeds off life."

My tattoo throbbed, and the moment my fingertips brushed over it, my mind echoed with memories of words I'd heard before.

To fight, to live

"To be Sídhe is to have life itself flowing in your blood." Keiri paused.

For a long while, we waited. Keiri said nothing. I felt more like I was taking a fairy philosophy class than like I was actually learning anything useful.

"What do you know about Olympus?"

Talk about an abrupt subject change. One moment it was all "to be Sídhe is to . . ." and the next, boom.

"Greek mythology." Zo sounded about as thrilled as I felt.

"Myths seldom get things right," Keiri said, "but they never get things entirely wrong."

"What myth are we talking about here?" Annabelle asked, always the one to ask the right question at the right time.

"You tell me," Keiri said. "It goes a little something like this." Suddenly, she seemed much more like a normal person, and much less like a crazy oracle-type. "Once upon a time, in a world not that far from our own, there were three young and powerful Sídhe children: two sisters, and a little boy whose life and destiny was tied to theirs. Some would call them fairies; some would call them gods.

"They were born in a time when fairy power was diminishing. The barrier between the worlds was becoming harder and harder to cross, and human life and Sídhe life were becoming so vastly different that the lines that connected them, the lines through which Sídhe power ran, were becoming thinner and thinner.

"And so these three children were born into the momentous task of closing the gap. They could see from

148

their world into ours, and they were to know human life, to know humans, and through their knowledge, the power inherent in all life was to return to the Sídhe.

"The two girls were as different as night and day. To the one went the task of knowing human life, and to the other, that of knowing human death."

Well that certainly sounded ominous.

"And so one watched humans live, and the other was with them in their moment of death, and as time went by, they crossed farther and farther from being observers to being something else altogether. Sister Life, as she was apt to call herself, began to weave the lines of human life, the very lines through which she got her power. It started with small things: making this person's lifeline cross that person's; lengthening this line or that; weaving together the lives of those she watched."

"And death?" Unlike me, Zo didn't squeak at all when she asked a question.

"Sister Death, who never called herself that, but nonetheless maintained the title among the Sídhe, was not enthralled with the lines the way her sister was. She knew the human race in death, knew it in war, and when the time came, she cut lifelines, undoing her sister's weaving and releasing the tension of life into the nothingness of death."

"What about the third?" I asked, managing a relatively squeak-free voice. "You said there were three."

"Birth," Delia said, answering for Keiri. All of us turned to look at her. "Duh," she said. "Was I the only one awake during Greek mythology? This is totally the fairy tale version of the three Fates."

The three Fates?

Adea.
Alecca.
Valgius.

Somehow, I'd never thought the three names together before, and the moment I did, the world around me blurred into a mess of colors and sounds, and then, there was nothing.

Chapter 13

"My love."

I turned in the direction of the bone-shattering voice. A man and a woman stood next to each other. His lips were so close to hers that I had to wonder if he was going to eat her alive. When she moved hers toward him, I grimaced and turned away. "Devour" probably would have been the appropriate word for what her lips did to his.

"I shouldn't be surprised."

At the sound of the new voice, I whirled around and found myself staring into startling blue eyes. I should have gotten used to eyes like those by now, but they weren't the kind of thing you could get used to.

"We spend our days with them, watching their lives, their deaths, their births, connecting ourselves to them so that our people may maintain their power, and this is what comes of it."

The two lovers broke away from each other.

"We know their loves, their hatred," the angry woman continued. Her hair was so blond that it shined like white silver in contrast to the lovers' darker hair. His was black, almost blue, and hers was a deep red, bordering on black.

Recognition shot through me, but I said nothing as I watched the drama before me unfold.

"We know what it is to be human, and our knowledge is the root of our power, and now, the two of you think you are *human*." The blond-haired girl plowed on. "You think you've fallen in love."

"We have," Adea spoke up, taking a step away from Valgius, her chin held high.

"We are not human, Adea. We do not love." There was something in her voice, in her tone, that made me wonder whether or not she really believed that; made me wonder if she'd ever loved.

Valgius stepped forward next to Adea. "We are Sídhe," he said simply, answering the allegations the third one had thrown at him. "We do that which we will."

The blond woman grinned, and though she was beautiful (totally centerfold material), it was a horrible sight. "You do your will," she said, "and I'll do mine."

"Alecca, we have not betrayed you." Adea's voice dropped to a whisper.

"No?" Alecca continued smiling. "There are three of us. There have always been three of us."

For a moment, I sympathized. She'd just found out that her sister and her best friend (possibly also her love interest?) were getting it on. Talk about being the third wheel. I tried to imagine Zo or Delia hooking up with Kane behind my back and physically shuddered.

"We were three," Alecca said, her tone for the first time almost sad. "And now?" She shook her head. "Now you have their love, and I have their hatred." Alecca laughed, cold, dry laughter that nearly split my head in two. "But one day, I'll have it all, and you, Adea, and you, Valgius, will bow before my power. You will have nothing, and I will have everything, and both worlds will fall at my feet."

"Not while I live," Adea said quietly.

"No," Alecca agreed. "That would hardly be an ending worthy of lovers such as you." She sneered. "Tragedy would suit better."

"You cannot kill us." Valgius sounded sure on this point.

Alecca held her hands up, and her whole body glowed with power. "You know each other," she said, taking a step forward with each word. "I know only them. How much more powerful, then, am I? I know them. I will absorb their lives into mine, and with their power, I will destroy you."

Adea and Valgius joined hands, and I had to look away from the light shining off their bodies.

Turning around and squinting into the light, I could see Alecca take a step backward.

"It doesn't have to be this way," Adea said softly. "Sister . . ."

"You will weaken without me," Alecca said through clenched teeth. "You will weaken and fade away. Without me, you will be nothing, and your love won't do a thing to save you. And just when you're most vulnerable, just when the balance of power begins to shift, there I'll be."

Startling blue eyes surged with fury, and though her voice was low, Alecca's next words sent a shiver racing up and down my spine at high frequency. "I will end you."

Alecca lashed out with one hand, and blood trickled down Adea's face, leaving a blue-green line in its wake.

"To destroy us would destroy the balance. Both worlds would be thrown into chaos. Sidhe, human . . ."

Alecca threw her hand through the air, cutting off her sister's plea. Valgius flew backward. He regained his footing, and made his own appeal.

"We are still three," he said.

Alecca stared at him for the longest moment, her blue eyes piercing his. "No," she said, and the quiet word screamed of betrayal and vengeance. "Never again." She advanced on them. Adea and Valgius began speaking in low tones as Alecca continued her onslaught, her fury slashing across their bodies, marking them with trails of blue-green blood. The lovers joined hands and continued chanting primal-sounding words I couldn't understand.

Alecca shook, but whether it was with anger, in fear, or from the power of their words, I couldn't tell. I could feel

the magic in the air, sizzling, pushing me back as Alecca
began her own chant.

"To earth I go
From air I breathe
I command myself
Unto the sea
For time unknown
The hate you've sown
Shall live in me
Until your weakness
Sets me free
And as I will
So mote it be."

Adea and Valgius kept chanting, the words persist-
ing against Alecca's in an odd rhythm. Power surged,
light flashed, and the world around me shook violently,
spastically.

And then they were gone.

"She does this sometimes."

As I came back into consciousness, I became quickly
aware of the fact that every inch of my body felt as if it
had been beaten from the inside out.

"My grandmother used to do this."

I opened my eyes. "I hate my life." I paused. "And
my body." I felt like throwing "and your grandmother"

on the end of that to Keiri, but somehow, that didn't seem like the best idea.

The first thing I saw was Keiri glaring at me, and I remembered a second too late that she was psychic.

"I saw them again," I said, more than ready to change the subject. "Only this time, they didn't see me."

I tried to sit up, but pain shot through my body, and a cry escaped my mouth.

"Bailey." Zo, Delia, and Annabelle were at my side in an instant.

"What's wrong?" Delia asked, panicked. "Are you hurt?"

Zo cursed under her breath.

"What did you see?" Annabelle and Keiri asked at the same time.

Great. Synchronized psychics.

"It was weird," I said, my voice hoarse from what I'd seen. "It was Adea and Valgius, and they were . . . kissing." That seemed like a nice way to put it. "And then . . ." It took me a moment to spit out her name. "Then Alecca saw them, and she was beyond ticked off, like they'd been doing it behind her back or something. And the way she looked at him, at both of them, it was like she'd been majorly betrayed. So Alecca goes off on this whole rant about how they aren't human and they're not supposed to love that way, and she threatens to kill them, even if it means destroying both worlds in the process. Or something like that."

"Wait a second," Delia said. "Are you telling me

that this whole apocalypse-y 'our lives, your fight, both worlds' thing started because of some kind of twisted fairy love triangle?"

I shrugged and nodded at the same time. "It's looking like a definite possibility."

"Sweet," Delia said.

All of us looked at her.

"Sweet?" Annabelle asked. "Sweet?"

"Not the whole whatever-it-takes, murderous part, but don't you think it's just a little bit cool that we're caught in the middle of some passionate cosmic affair?"

"Trust me," I told her. "It didn't feel cool."

"Soap opera." That was Zo, who folded her arms over her chest, still keeping an eagle eye on me lying on the sofa. "I told you. Greek mythology: one giant soap opera."

"It doesn't seem that much like Greek mythology," Annabelle, who was in all likelihood an expert on Greek mythology, said skeptically.

"Myths," Keiri said, shaking her head. "If it wasn't for people like my grandmother, and Bailey, we'd probably never have known."

"This is just a temporary gig," I said. "It came with the tattoo, and believe me, if I'd known what I was getting myself into . . ."

"You mean you don't know?" Keiri asked.

I stared at her.

"That's Bailey's clueless face," Delia clarified for the older woman.

"I assumed that you knew. There are so few Guardian lines left these days, and—"

"Guardian lines?" all of us asked at once.

"Blessed Ones," Keiri said impatiently. "Those touched by the Sídhe, chosen to guard their heirlooms and powers in this world to maintain the great balance."

I stared at her. Great balance? Heirlooms? Blessed? As if.

"Your dreams are Sídhe-blocked," Keiri told me. "I can't read them, and I'm betting your friend there can't, either."

I purposefully didn't look at Annabelle, who'd told me from the start that my dreams were a mystery to her.

"But you can't read Annabelle, either," I said in my own defense.

"Right," Keiri said, as if I'd just made a point in *her* favor. "I can't read Annabelle at all, which tells me there's some kind of external magic at play. I'm far too strong for a noninitiated mortal to block me completely."

Was it me, or did Keiri say "mortal" as though she . . . well, as though she wasn't one?

"The women in my family were once priestesses at the Sídhe temples." Keiri answered the question I hadn't had the guts to voice. "Guardians of their secrets, owners of objects that they passed from their realm into ours."

"Blessed," Annabelle said.

Keiri nodded. "The Sídhe smiled upon the Guardians and blessed them. Touched them. Trace amounts of their power leaked into our blood. My daughter and I are the last of an ancient line of Guardians. We are blessed. Short of some kind of Sídhe magic intervening, I should be able to read all of you."

"That's Bailey's clueless face again," Delia piped up. I was starting to wonder if I had any other face.

"Annabelle isn't blocking me." Keiri spelled it out. "Something else is blocking me from reading Annabelle. A totem, a spell, I don't know what, but Annabelle's mind is well hidden behind some kind of outside mystical veil. Bailey, you, on the other hand, are an open book." She smiled at me. "Your thoughts practically broadcast themselves over a loudspeaker, and yet, when it comes to your dream-visions, the voices you hear, I get nothing." She paused. "It's not a broad enough block to be coming from outside magic. *You're* blocking me."

"Maybe someone else doesn't want you to see the dreams, and they're blocking you," I said reasonably. I was being the reasonable one here. Tattoo mojo aside, people just weren't descended from fairy-touched Guardian chicks, and even if they were, I certainly wasn't. That was crazy.

This coming from the girl who heard voices, I reminded myself.

"Besides the blocking, there are other clues." Keiri plowed on. "Your hair, for one."

"Not my actual color," I said quickly. "And for the record, not my shirt either."

Keiri turned to Delia. "Could you change her hair

back?" she asked. "I've gotten a visual of her natural color from your minds, but I'd like to be sure."

With a surprisingly small amount of grumbling, Delia lifted her hands to my head and changed my hair back to its normal color.

"It's bicolored hair," Keiri said. "Not one color streaked with another, but actually two different colors in one."

I fingered my not-blond, not-brown hair. I'd always hated it.

"It's the mark of the Sídhe," Keiri said, "and those chosen from birth by their ancient magic."

I opened my mouth to protest, but a strong visual hopped into my mind. Adea, with her red-black hair, arm in arm with a blue-black-haired Valgius. I chewed on the inside of my lip. Alecca's hair had been silver-blond.

It's in the blood, it is. Things of power always are.

"Bailey?" Annabelle spoke up. "When did you say the first time you heard the voices was?"

"When I saw the tattoos." I said without thinking. "Sídhe blue, blood green." I remembered the words I'd heard, saying them out loud.

"And the room went all funky-like when I put on my tattoo, right?" Delia asked.

I nodded. "So?"

"Bailey, that was *before* you put on your tattoo."

I opened my mouth and then closed it again. They were right. I'd heard the voices before I'd ever put on my tattoo, and if our powers did come from the tattoos, then . . .

"It's in the blood," I said out loud. "Valgius, it was something he kept saying, about the power being the blood." I paused. "I thought he meant his blood and our powers, but maybe he meant *my* blood." I gulped. "My blessed blood."

Delia lifted her arms above her head in an impromptu stretch, and Keiri's eyes went immediately to her stomach.

"Or maybe," Keiri said, her eyes locked on the tattoo, "he meant both." She leaned forward and ran a finger over the edge of Delia's tattoo.

Delia squirmed. "No touchy," she protested. "That tickles."

"The power is in the blood," Keiri said. "Of course."

"Care to let us in on that 'of course'?" Zo asked. I thought she was restraining herself quite nicely, all things considered.

"I'd wondered how they managed to give you all such strong powers. Sídhe powers." Keiri finally tore her eyes off Delia's stomach. "It's their blood."

"What's their blood?" Delia asked suspiciously.

I answered for Keiri. "The tattoos." I took a deep and only somewhat cleansing breath. "I keep seeing that color everywhere, whenever any of us uses our powers." It all clicked into place. "Sídhe blue, blood green," I babbled on. "Don't you get it?" I didn't wait for anyone to answer. "And when Alecca made Adea bleed, she . . ."

"She what?" Now it was Delia's turn to squeak.

"Her blood was the color of our tattoos," I said.

"It was a transfer of power by blood," Keiri said, her eyes sparkling with the very idea of it. "Their blood, applied to your skin."

"I'd like to take a moment to ewwwwwwwww." Delia wrinkled her nose. "I don't want some guy's blood all over me. I don't care if he is a fairy king."

"It's not *all* over you," Zo said, half to comfort Delia and half to torment her. As for me, at this point, there wasn't much that could surprise me.

I was descended from people who'd been literally and mystically touched by fairies? Sure.

I was wearing fairy blood on my back? Okay.

An evil fairy who may or may not have been one of the three Fates was on some kind of murderous power trip just because she'd ended up on the wrong vertex of a love triangle? Why the hell not?

I tried not to think it. Every part of me that had ever seen a scary movie absolutely forbade me from thinking it. I was determined not to think it. And yet . . .

"What next?"

Chapter 14

It took Annabelle all of about thirty seconds to shove a pen and paper into my hands.

"I don't even know if I can move," I said. That last dream-vision, or whatever Keiri had called it, had taken a lot out of me. Actually, that was an understatement. That last dream-vision had kicked my butt and then gone all kamikaze on the rest of me.

Keiri put her hands on my shoulders.

I stared back at her, more than a little uncomfortable. I barely knew this woman. Granted, I was lying on her couch and she apparently knew more about my long-past family history than I did, but still.

"Relax," Keiri said, and I felt myself instantly relaxing. Was she pulling an Annabelle on me? The next second, I didn't care, because slowly, the pain trickled out of my body like water off an icicle.

"What was that?" I asked when she was finished.

Keiri shrugged. "Let's just say that my Guardian gifts extend beyond mind reading."

As casually as I could, I got a good look at her hair. It was dark, somewhere between brown and black. Or maybe, I thought, it actually was both.

I didn't say anything, even though I was pretty sure that Annabelle, Keiri, and the entire psychic population of the Western Hemisphere were picking up my thoughts. Instead, I took the pen Annabelle had given me and started writing down everything I could remember about the argument between Adea, Valgius, and Alecca.

"You know anything else useful?" Zo asked Keiri bluntly as I wrote.

Keiri didn't seem put off by Zo's tone. "More?" she asked. "I told you what I knew of Adea's origins, and the mechanism through which you received your powers. What more can I tell you?"

"Do you know what our symbols mean?" Annabelle asked. "I have a linguist looking into them, but anything you can tell us would be greatly appreciated."

"May I see?" Keiri asked.

Without a word, Annabelle slipped her barrette out of her hair, turned around, and lifted her hair off her neck, baring her tattoo.

"It's a symbol associated with Adea," Keiri said.

164

"I'm not sure what it means, only that my grandmother carved it into a tree in her backyard when she was a young girl."

"We saw it on the website," Delia volunteered helpfully.

"I asked the webmistress to add it to their website— my best effort at luring in anyone who had any actual information on Adea after I discovered that the Daughters of Adea weren't quite what I had hoped them to be." Keiri paused and then spoke again. "Yes, perhaps I did hope too much."

At the exact same moment, Annabelle's and Keiri's eyebrows shot into their hairlines.

"Did you just—"

"Yes, I did."

"And the block?"

"Gone."

I was having a little trouble following, and I wasn't the only one.

"Care to share with the class, girls?" Zo asked.

"Annabelle wondered if I'd hoped too much of the Daughters," Keiri said. "It just took me a moment to realize that she'd wondered it silently."

"She read my mind," Annabelle said. She wrinkled her forehead. "She made her way through my block somehow." The idea that someone might actually be reading her mind clearly concerned Annabelle.

"Welcome to my world," Zo told her gleefully, reading her cousin's face as well as I was.

"I didn't fight through the block," Keiri said. "It's gone."

"How?" Annabelle asked doubtfully. "How can it have just disappeared? You said there was a powerful, external magical force at play." Still in a bit of a huff, she straightened her hair, securing it over her tattoo with the barrette.

Immediately, Keiri reached for Annabelle's hand. "And now you're gone again," she said. "I can't hear you."

Annabelle, her hand still on the barrette, unclipped it and drew it back. "What about now?" she asked.

Keiri nodded. "You're back," she said.

All of us looked at the barrette in Annabelle's hand.

"Old-fashioned, but a nice accent piece," Delia commented. "Where'd you get that, anyway?"

I knew the exact moment the answer dawned on Annabelle. Her mouth dropped open slightly and her eyebrows shot up. "At the booth at the mall," she said, "where we got the tattoos."

"It's magicked," Keiri said quickly. "Powerful magic. Sídhe magic."

I thought of the woman who'd sold the tattoos to us. She'd had blue eyes. Eyes like Adea, Valgius, and Alecca. Eyes the color that Delia had turned mine that morning. Who was she? Yet another question to add to my ever-growing list.

"Why couldn't I have gotten the mind-blocking barrette?" Zo asked, scuffing her foot into the ground.

"You don't wear barrettes," Delia said, as if it was

the most obvious thing in the world. "It's totally not suited to your style." Delia paused. "Excuse me, your 'style.' " She added air quotes the second time around, trying to distract Zo from the fact that she'd yet again gotten the short straw in the power lottery.

"It's not like Annabelle even really needs it," Zo said. "You never have any incriminating thoughts, Anna—"

"Here, let me show you something," Keiri interrupted Zo. She left the room and returned a moment later holding a small, clear crystal in her hand. Upon closer inspection, I noticed that it was attached to a translucent cord.

"What is it about me that screams 'give me a crystal'?" Zo asked.

"Your tomboy pastiche?" Delia guessed.

Keiri bit back a smile. "Or it could be the fact that those gifted with premonition are often also given divination," she said, "and that Annabelle, as a psychic, would be the most dangerous to have an open mind, since she'd have already compiled everything important that the rest of you have been thinking." Keiri shrugged. "Just a thought."

"What's 'divination'?" Zo asked, intrigued at the idea that she might actually have another power.

"Divination actually just means finding," Keiri said. "In some circles, it's another word for premonition. If one goes looking for the future, through tea leaves or palm reading or tarot cards, then that's divination. At least, if they do it successfully and they find the future,

167

it's divination. Otherwise, it's just tea leaves." Seeing Zo's look, Keiri got back on track. "If your premonition stems from an underlying power of divination, then you might be able to use that power toward another end."

"You mean she could find stuff other than the future?" Delia asked.

Keiri nodded.

"And that has to do with the crystals how?" Zo asked. Keiri was winning Zo over despite herself.

"Crystals are often used in scrying," Keiri explained. "If you're looking for something in a small terrain, such as your bedroom . . ."

Or your kitchen, I added silently. How had Zo known her dad had left the pizza money in a drawer underneath a notepad? How had she known it wasn't on *top* of the notepad?

". . . in small terrain, such as your bedroom, you might be able to divine for an object without working with any medium. You may simply sense its location, but when you're working on finding something, or someone, over a larger space, say a city, then scrying would probably be a diviner's best bet."

Keiri held the crystal out at arm's length and let it drop. She held on to the cord, and the crystal wobbled back and forth. After a moment, she handed the cord to Zo. "If you hold it over a map," she said, "and concentrate on your target, it should stop swinging over the correct location, allowing you to pinpoint your target."

"So she's kind of like a human lost and found," Delia said brightly.

"If her premonition does in fact stem from a greater power of divination," Keiri said, "then yes."

Zo eyed the crystal warily. "All right," she said after a moment. "Might as well give it a try."

By that time, my hand hurt from the fast and furious writing I'd been doing, and I set the pen down. "What are you going to find?" I asked her.

"Let's try something simple," Keiri said. Her eyes scanned the room, and then she picked up the pair of earrings on the coffee table. "Close your eyes," she told Zo.

Surprisingly, Zo complied without so much as a single sarcastic comment or eye roll. Silently, Keiri leaned over and slipped one of the earrings into the front pocket of my jeans, and then handed the second one to Annabelle, who stuck it to the back of one of the couch pillows.

"Now concentrate," Keiri said, her voice soft and lilting. "Think of the earrings. Where are they?"

"In Bay's pocket on the back of the couch," Zo replied without pausing. Then she wrinkled her forehead. "One's in Bailey's pocket," she corrected herself. "The other one's on the back of the pillow behind Annabelle."

She opened her eyes.

Without a word, I handed her the earring from my pocket.

"What about the scrying thing?" Delia asked. "Do you have a map, Keiri?"

Five minutes later, at Delia's insistence, Zo was swinging the crystal over a map of the city, scrying for hot guys. Every once in a while, the crystal would change directions, pulled to a particular area of the map like a magnet to metal.

"Try something more specific," Keiri suggested.

"Like a particular hot guy?" Delia asked.

Annabelle rolled her eyes.

Delia grinned impishly at me. "Scry for Kane," she said.

Zo laughed out loud and complied. She swung the crystal gently over the map, counterclockwise. I watched it, my mind on Kane. And Kane's eyes. And Kane's arms.

And Kane's mouth.

Without warning, the crystal jerked to a stop at the intersection of Whaley and Vermuse.

"Found him," Zo said, wiggling her eyebrows at me. "Looks like he's at the school." As soon as the word "school" left her mouth, Zo's jaw clenched tight. Her head flew back with such force that I was afraid she'd snapped her neck, and she sank down to all fours, the cord attached to the crystal still firmly clasped in her hand. Even without tension in the cord, the crystal stood on its end, pointing to the exact location of the high school.

At my feet, Zo shuddered, and I bent down and rubbed my hand down her back. "Zo," I said softly. "Zo?"

She was too deeply absorbed in the vision to hear me.

"Leave her be," Keiri said. "She'll come back to us once she's seen what she was meant to see."

When Zo finally did sit up and open her eyes, the four of us stared at her, waiting.

"Dance." The first word out of Zo's mouth wasn't anywhere near what I'd expected.

"You want us to dance?" Delia asked, clearly perplexed.

Zo, her face ashen, shook her head. "No," she said, her voice catching in her throat. "School dance."

Delia grinned. "Now this is what I'm talking about," she said. "It's about time we started getting something out of these premonitions of yours. What was everyone wearing? Who was Kane dancing with? Is my date hot? Do you come to your senses and buy that dress at Escape? Is there a lot of black or is it more . . ." At the look on Zo's face, Delia finally trailed off. "Oh," she said glumly. "Not a happy dance vision?"

"Not a happy dance vision," I confirmed on Zo's behalf.

"What happened?" Annabelle voiced the question I couldn't seem to make my mouth form.

"One minute, I was staring at the map and the crystal was hovering over the school, and the next . . ." Zo met my eyes, only mine. "I was there, at the dance.

There were these lame crepe-paper decorations, and the music was completely ridiculous, and the people . . ."

"Were being chain-saw-massacred?" Delia guessed, completely seriously.

Zo rolled her eyes, and I breathed a sigh of relief. If she was back to rolling her eyes at Delia, she was okay. "Not chain-saw-massacred," Zo said. "One second they were dancing, and the next they were on the ground."

Somehow, that so wasn't what I'd expected to hear.

"It started slowly. Marissa Baker, you know, the goody-goody newspaper chick? Well, she was taking people's pictures, and then, right in the middle of shooting a bunch of couples dancing, she fell, no warning, to the ground. Nobody noticed. Nobody."

Marissa Baker was the kind of person people didn't notice at dances.

"And then . . . what's the kid's name? The one with the really thick glasses and the greasy part?"

I racked my mind for a name, but I couldn't seem to remember it, even though he sat behind me in homeroom.

"He asks Jessie Perkins to dance, and she's about to blow him off, and then he falls over, and she just steps right over him."

As I contemplated the fact that Jessie, like her BFF (Alex Atkins), was evil, Zo continued rattling off names of kids.

"And then they were all dropping at once, and people finally started noticing when Alex dropped. . . ."

Alex? I couldn't imagine her falling like the others. Alex Atkins didn't have a weakness, just like she didn't have a functional heart or any kind of conscience. I had serious doubts about whether she actually even needed to eat or sleep.

"Everyone started screaming, and the more they screamed, the more of them fell unconscious to the floor, completely still. And pale."

Zo's voice was matter-of-fact now, and she was pretending that what she was saying didn't bother her at all, but Keiri was psychic, and the rest of us knew Zo too well to buy her tough-guy act.

"Anything else?" Annabelle asked. I could tell by the tone of her voice that it was taking great restraint on her part to abstain from forcing Zo to write down an alphabetized victim list.

Zo nodded. "There was a woman there. Sort of." Zo shook her head and let her blond hair fall in her face. "She was sort of there, and sort of not."

Alecca. I knew before Zo described the woman she'd seen that it would be her.

"Light hair, dark lips." Zo paused, and I knew what was coming next. "Blue, blue eyes."

"Alecca." This time, I forced myself to say her name out loud. "But why? What's she doing to them, and why kids?"

I couldn't help but remember her words. *I will absorb their lives into mine, and with their power, I will destroy you.*

"Power." Keiri answered my question, even as my memory did the same. "There's power in life," she said simply. "Especially in young life. If Alecca found some way to absorb part of her victims' life forces into her own, she could amass tremendous amounts of power."

The power to kill Adea and Valgius. I'd seen Alecca's eyes when she'd found them together. Something told me that a couple of millennia under the sea hadn't made her change her mind about the whole destroy-them-at-all-costs thing.

Annabelle's phone buzzed, breaking our silence, and when she glanced at the incoming number, she took in an audible breath. "Lionel," she told us.

"Our linguist," Delia told Keiri, the way any other fashionista would have said "my stylist" or "my masseuse."

"Answer it," I told Annabelle. While she talked, I turned back to Zo.

"The dance is tomorrow night," I said, sounding way more confident than I felt. "If we stop Alecca before then, none of this will ever happen." Secretly, I wondered what "all of this" entailed. Were people just passed out, or were they . . . I couldn't even force my mind to say it, but seeing Alecca as I had, knowing her as I did, I had to wonder if she'd stop at absorbing part of a person's life force when she could go for the whole thing. She hadn't seemed bothered at all by the fact that killing Adea and Valgius might somehow mess up her

174

world and ours. It was hard to imagine that she'd care any more about a single human life.

"Then we stop Alecca before tomorrow night," Zo said, her voice leaving no room for argument.

I couldn't tell her what I knew about Alecca; couldn't tell her what I thought she might have seen.

"We stop her before tomorrow night." I said what Zo needed to hear, but as much as I hated to admit it, it seemed impossible. We didn't know where Alecca was, or even really what she was capable of doing. We didn't know how she went about attacking people, or if Marissa, Alex, and company were her first victims. We knew nothing, and I couldn't shake the feeling that I was missing the most obvious piece of the whole puzzle.

"Lionel has some news for us." Annabelle's voice broke into my inner depressothon.

"Did he decode the symbols already?" Delia asked. "Isn't that like incredibly fast?"

"He wouldn't tell me over the phone," Annabelle said with a frown, "but he sounded really excited. He said I'd have to see it to believe it, said that he woke up in the middle of the night last night with an idea and had been working on it ever since."

"Old guy's going to give himself a heart attack," Zo said halfheartedly. The vision had taken even more out of her than she was letting on, and I wondered if she was holding something back.

"Don't we already know what the symbols mean?" I

asked Annabelle, forcing my mind to the problem at hand. "Mine's fire, somehow yours is mind reading, Zo's is future telling, and Delia's is changing stuff."

As I named our powers, I couldn't help but wonder what we were supposed to do with them. Stop Alecca, obviously, but . . .

"That's just it," Annabelle said. "Lionel doesn't think they're just self-contained symbols."

"What does he think they are?" Zo asked.

Annabelle leaned forward, and for a moment, I wondered if there was even the slightest chance that a linguistic revelation could change the incredible odds stacked against us.

"Lionel doesn't think they're self-contained symbols," Annabelle said again. She paused. "He thinks it's a prophecy."

Chapter 15

Fifteen minutes later, I was sure of exactly one thing. You could always count on Delia in a crisis. You could count on her to remain utterly and completely unfazed no matter what happened.

"I'm just saying," Delia said. "This whole prophecy thing is going to tell us everything we need to know, so you three should just stop worrying and concentrate on the fact that we're headed to a college campus, and Zo could totally scry for hot, single guys who would love to go to a high school dance." Delia was the eternal optimist. In her mind, we'd already as good as beaten the bad guy, so she'd moved on to other important issues.

"We don't even have a map," I said, not wanting to point out the more obvious: that we didn't know what, if anything, this whole prophecy thing was going to tell us.

"I'm sure we can get a map if we really need one," Delia said, undeterred. "Or can't you just, you know, concentrate on thinking about hot guys?"

If anything was going to help Zo recover from the crippling vision of doom, it was Delia being one hundred percent Delia.

"Annabelle?" Sensing that I wasn't going to be any help, Zo turned to her cousin.

Annabelle held my gaze for a second and then nodded. I got the message: until we knew what was in this prophecy, obsessing over Zo's vision and Monday's dance wasn't going to help any of us.

"College boys," Annabelle mused. Even A-belle, queen of common sense, had her weak points. "Prophecy first," she said as we entered the linguistics building. "Then boys."

Hearing the word "prophecy" made me feel really conspicuous. People in real life didn't just run into prophecies on a day-to-day basis. This wasn't *Buffy*, our library wasn't stocked crazy-full of ancient scrolls, and people definitely didn't encode prophecies in fake tattoos. Honestly, what were the chances?

"Given the events of the past couple of days," Annabelle replied to my unspoken question, "pretty good."

"How's Lionel even sure it's a prophecy?" I asked. "I mean, couldn't it just be a sentence?"

"I wonder if prophecies are like fortune cookies,"

Delia mused. "You know, how you're supposed to add 'in bed' to the end of the fortune cookie. Think the same goes for prophecies?"

"What?" Annabelle asked. I couldn't believe that she'd never heard the fortune cookie thing before. The rest of us had been doing it since the beginning of freshman year.

Delia explained patiently, her mind, for the moment, off of scrying for boys. "Like if a fortune cookie says 'you will discover a new talent,' then you read the fortune cookie as 'you will discover a new talent in bed.' A fortune cookie's kind of like a prophecy." Delia paused. "Don't you think?"

Zo snorted for the first time since her last vision. "The world is going to end . . . ," she said in a deep voice.

". . . in bed," Delia and I added at once. Zo grinned. Delia had managed to snap her (and me for that matter) out of it.

"Beware the evil fairy . . ."

". . . in bed."

"And the true king will pull the sword from the stone . . ." Annabelle was finally getting into the spirit of things. "In bed."

"Doesn't have quite the same ring." Delia looked so honestly thoughtful that I couldn't help myself. Soon, we were caught up in a fit of giggles. We slumped against the wall outside Lionel's office, trying to collect ourselves, but every time I managed to catch my breath, one of them would mutter "in bed," and I'd be gone all over again. I blame hysteria. We were standing right smack in between a horrible, albeit cryptic, vision and a mysterious prophecy. It was either goofiness or depression, and Delia's optimism was catching. On some level, I felt like if I just let things get back to normal—joking, laughing, making a fool of myself—then everything would be okay. Alecca wouldn't be planning what I feared she was planning, and the whole dance thing would take care of itself.

"Annie, you're here." The sound of Lionel's voice had me choking back the last of my laughter, but I could feel it sitting in the back of my throat, ready to bubble over with the least bit of provocation. That or I'd burst into tears. At this point, I wasn't going to rule out any possibility.

"Come look at what Lionel has to show you." The old man grinned so broadly that I thought he was going to hurt himself.

My mouth dropped open the second I stepped into his office. Hundreds of pieces of paper flooded his desk and avalanched onto the floor. I could make out drawings on some, scribblings on others. The walls, too, were plastered with sketches of our tattoos and other symbols I didn't recognize.

If I hadn't been there the day before, I would have thought this was the office of an insane person. An obsessed person.

"I couldn't sleep," Lionel said. "I kept thinking

about the shapes, the twists and turns, the way that all of the symbols appeared both pictorial and textual in nature." He adjusted his glasses. "I'd put in an e-mail to a friend about the symbol in the book, hoping that he'd have some information on the druidic language the symbol is rooted in, but still, I couldn't shake the feeling that I was missing something." The words tumbled out, and I was half afraid that the old guy was going to give himself a heart attack.

Picking up a pen, he grabbed a fresh sheet of paper and drew our symbols onto it by heart. As he spoke, he traced the curves and lines of their forms over and over again. "Pictorial and textual, druidic, and yet there was something almost like Chinese characters about them. I'd look at them and see bits and pieces, elements of Egyptian, Japanese, Greek, and indigenous languages scattered as far as Peru and Alaska—"

"Lionel," Annabelle broke in gently. I guess she was starting to have heart attack phobia as well.

"Then I fell asleep." Lionel gestured toward his desk.

"You fell asleep here?" I asked.

Lionel nodded. "I forgot the time," he said, "and when I woke up, I had a moment of extreme clarity. Had I been fully conscious, I would have dismissed the thought as ludicrous. A linguistic impossibility."

"But you didn't," Annabelle said slowly.

"That I didn't, Annie." Lionel's eyes sparkled. "That I didn't. Instead, still half-asleep, I gave it a try."

"Gave what a try?" Zo blurted out. She was clearly having as much trouble following the sleep-deprived linguist's rantings as I was.

Lionel gestured to the drawings that covered the walls and floor. "It took me a bit," he said, "but I was convinced the right combinations were here somewhere."

"Combinations?" Annabelle tilted her head to the side.

"What if," Lionel said, "what if the symbols weren't just druidic? What if the reason I saw so many languages in them, the reason the set seemed so broad, was that the symbols were actually many languages?"

Now, I didn't have a background in linguistics, but I was pretty sure that what he was saying didn't make any sense. One look at Annabelle confirmed what I was thinking.

"You don't believe me, I see, my girl," Lionel said, tweaking Annabelle's hair. "Nor should you, until you see what I have to show." Delicately, he picked up a stack of transparencies off his desk. "Several hours in, I realized that this way might be easier, not to mention environmentally friendlier than using paper." Carefully, he spread the transparencies apart. On each of them, he'd drawn one of our symbols.

"By this time, I'd gotten the rough translations of the symbols themselves," he said, as if that was of no importance at all.

"What are they?" I tried to keep my voice soothing and calm.

Lionel pointed to each of them as he spoke. "Fire. Knowledge. Future. Metamorphosis."

Come to think of it, Delia's tattoo had always kind of looked like a half butterfly.

"But that is unimportant," Lionel said. "What is interesting is what happens when you superimpose the symbols." Gingerly, he lifted my symbol and put it on top of Annabelle's. "Apart, you get druidic symbols of obscure meanings, but together . . ." Sitting on top of Annabelle's, parts of my symbol disappeared, aligning exactly with hers, forming a new shape altogether. "It's a Sumerian character meaning life," Lionel said.

Annabelle gawked at him.

"Don't give me that look, my dear. It's all perfectly verifiable." He tweaked the end of her nose. "Just watch." He switched the transparencies around, turning Annabelle's upside down and placing it over Zo's. "Japanese," he said as the lines of Zo's symbol crossed Annabelle's. "Or rather an Indo-Japanese precursor, but that's not the point. The point is, combined this way, the symbols take on a new meaning." He paused, looking at each of us in turn. "A new meaning in an entirely new language." I thought the old man was going to break into a dance of glee. "Any way you combine the symbols, you get a valid, though often obscure, character from a *different* extinct, ancient language."

Zo let out a low whistle. "That's some pretty crazy stuff," she said.

Lionel boomed with laughter. "That it is," he said. "That it is."

I cleared my throat. So far, all we had was one character that meant life, and that didn't seem entire-school-dying-level bad. Maybe Alex and company were just a little light-headed. I clung to the idea as I pushed on. "Annabelle said you thought it was a prophecy," I said. "What does it say?"

"Perhaps I spoke too soon," Lionel said. "I was overexcited by the discovery and conjectured that anything put so thoroughly in code that spoke of life and death could well be of a prophetic nature."

"Life and death?" I asked.

He nodded, and took out six new drawings: each one a combination of two of our tattoo symbols. "Life and death. Battle. Spider or web, the translation is ambiguous on that one. End. Soul."

Hadn't Zo said something about a sentence? That didn't sound sentencelike to me.

"These concepts can obviously be combined in a variety of novel ways," Lionel said. "For example, one such reading might be, 'in the end battle, the soul will be in the web of life and death,' or 'the battle of the soul of death will end the spider's life.' You see?"

Life. Death. Battle. Spider. End. Soul.

"What if you combine the combinations?" Delia was the first to recover her voice.

Lionel looked at her, surprised. "I hadn't tried that," he said, "but with six combinations there and with the number of archaic languages possible, it could take quite a bit of time."

I scratched my fingernail lightly over the tattoo on my back.

Life and death, death and life.

"What if you just combine life and death?" I asked. Lionel did as I asked, and there, all four of our symbols sat on top of each other. Lionel opened a book and started flipping through it. "Tathuvian? Nalagasi? Honduit?" He rattled off the nonsense-sounding words. I was guessing they were more obscure archaic languages, though it honestly sounded like gibberish to me.

"Balance." Lionel closed the book and slumped over on his desk. "It means balance."

"Balance," Delia repeated.

Time runs thin.

"No time," I said out loud.

The other three looked at me.

"It *is* getting kind of late," Zo said. "And we do have that thing with needing to be in before dark."

"We have time," Annabelle said. "Not a lot, but plenty to get home and then some to spare."

Time runs thin.

Sheesh. Persistent little voices, weren't they? Did they think I didn't realize that we had less than twenty-four hours until the dance of doom? No matter how hard I laughed or tried to forget about it, I couldn't.

The very conspicuous sound of snoring broke me from my thoughts. There, in the middle of a stack of papers, Lionel had fallen asleep, and somehow, he was managing to make more noise asleep than he had awake.

Very sweetly, Annabelle leaned forward and pressed a small kiss to his cheek. "Thank you, Lionel," she said.

The rest of us took that as our cue to exit.

"The battle of life and death ends the spider soul." Zo tried out variations on the words. "The spider battles the end of life and death."

"You forgot soul," I said.

Zo snorted. "Fine. The soul spider battles the end of life and death," she said, sticking "soul" in at random.

"No," Delia corrected with a weak smile. "The soul spider battles the end of life and death in bed."

For a split second, there was silence, and then I felt the giggles pouring out of my mouth. It made no sense. The prophecy that was supposed to solve all of our problems made no sense. It shouldn't have been funny.

And yet, it was.

"In bed," Zo agreed with a grin, and just when she was starting to return to her normal self, her head was flung back against the wall. Her eyes glazed over, and another vision took hold of her body. Moving quickly, Annabelle grabbed her cousin's shoulders, steadying her while the premonition ran its course.

I gritted my teeth, watching Zo's body shudder with the power of what she was seeing. Was it me, or were these things getting more and more violent? When Zo's body finally stopped trembling, she met me with eyes on the verge of tearing over. "A little boy," she managed.

"Eight or nine. He was taking a bath, and then he lifted his eyes to the ceiling and just stared." She paused. "He was thinking about Little League and sloshing water over the side because he was mad at his mom, and the next second, he was humming and staring, staring and humming, and . . ."

Delia took a step toward Zo and grabbed her hand. Zo held on tightly. "He just hummed and stared and went under." Her words hung in the air. "And he stayed under, staring up through the water with these horrible blue eyes until he drowned."

First our entire school falling to the floor (dead?) with no warning, and now this—a little kid, humming and staring like Amber. I couldn't shake the image of the smoky gray tentacles from my mind. Were they there in the bathroom Zo had seen, pulling the boy out of his body?

Were they in the auditorium, pulling our classmates out of their bodies?

For the first time, it occurred to me that maybe Zo had been getting premonitions about Alecca from the start. Amber. The dance. Now.

"Where?" Annabelle asked the question quietly.

"I need a map," Zo said, "and I need one now." She turned away, but I saw her drag the back of her hand across her face, roughly brushing off the single tear running down her cheek.

Time runs thin.

Right now, that was the last thing I needed to hear. I

looked out the window. The sun was still largely visible on the horizon, but I knew that we only had about forty-five minutes of sunlight left.

Without a word, I followed Zo in her hot pursuit of a map. Right now, there was only one thing that mattered, and it wasn't time.

Chapter 16

The glare on Zo's face was starting to take on a life of its own. Any second now, I expected it to rush to the front of the bus and throttle the bus driver for daring to slow down and pick up more passengers when we were obviously in a hurry.

"That's it." Zo charged up to the front of the bus.

"What's she doing?" Delia asked warily.

Without a word, Zo stomped down the steps and off the bus.

"But we're still two stops away," Annabelle said. "She can't possibly think we'll get there faster on foot."

Zo put her hands on her hips and stared up, daring us to argue.

"Gonna go out on a limb here and guess that she can," I said, and with a sigh, I got up from my seat, squeezed my way down the aisle, and went to stand next to Zo. Delia and Annabelle were right behind me.

On the horizon, the sun was just starting to set.

"Four blocks," Zo said, and that was the only explanation any of us got before she took off running.

"The running thing?" Delia said. "It gets really old."

I had to agree, but I couldn't shake the image of the gray tentacles pulling the life out of a little boy. Somehow, my antirunning feelings didn't really weigh in.

We'd made it about half a block before Delia's eyes lit up. Without so much as a word to me, she wiggled her fingers at my shoes. "Rollerblades."

"Aaaaaaaaaaaaaaaaaaaaaaaaaccckkkkkkkk!"

As my shoes morphed underneath me, I started to lose my balance, and by the time I caught it, I was skating at top speed toward Zo, who had at least half a block on me. Moments later, Annabelle and Delia were skating at my side.

"You couldn't have thought of this the last three times we were running?" I huffed. "And what about giving a girl a little warning? You almost killed me!"

Delia flipped her hair behind her shoulder. "You're welcome," she said pointedly.

As I skated, the wind in my face, closer and closer to the address Zo had pinpointed as the boy's location, the sound of my own heart beating grew louder and louder in my ears. We were skating toward something, I could feel it; something I didn't want to see. Something that we weren't ready for.

Alecca.

Was it really her? Had she attacked Amber? Was she attacking this little boy?

As if from a great distance, I could hear Delia prattling on to Annabelle about designer Rollerblades, but soon, my mind drowned out everything except the sound of my own beating heart and the feel of the wind on my face. Under my skin, blood surged through my veins.

The blood runs thin.

My heart pumped, the blood coursed through my flesh. The wind beat against my face.

Blood. Blood. Blood. It's in the blood.

Slowly, the sound of my beating heart changed, taking on a new rhythm until, finally, I could hear the soft, sweet sound of low-pitched humming. The eerie, almost intoxicatingly simple tune grew louder and louder with each beat of my heart.

It took me a moment to realize that I was skating toward the sound.

Two voices hummed in unison: one young and high, and the other so pure and ancient that just the sound of it hurt my bones. Louder and louder, faster and faster, the voices grew, until there was only one voice. That voice.

I flashed back, seeing Amber as she'd been on the balcony: eyes looking at something no one else could see, humming a song that no one else could hear.

The song rolled over me and got fainter and fainter,

until it was replaced again by the sound of my own rapidly beating heart.

Blood. Blood. Blood.

I could feel my breathing quicken, and as the world came back into focus, I concentrated on not blading straight into a quickly approaching mailbox. My heart quieted, but I could still feel the blood coursing through my veins.

Blood recognizes blood.

"OMG." Delia's tone was almost flat.

"What?" I asked. She didn't respond, and in the next instant, I heard the sirens.

As we rounded the corner, I ran smack into Zo, taking her down to the ground with me as I fell. She didn't move, and for the longest time, we just lay there, our limbs entangled and our eyes locked on the ambulance in the driveway.

"No," Zo said finally, her voice calm and stubborn. "We can still make it."

My whole body numb, I followed her toward the house. She was right. The boy couldn't be gone already. I'd heard him humming; I was sure of it. The humming had only just stopped. How could they have called an ambulance already? How long had I been absorbed in the sound of the humming, the intoxicating rush of my own blood?

The moment Zo stepped foot on the sidewalk in front of the house, she skidded to a stop, her feet frozen to the ground and her body stiff. I grabbed her arms and found myself in the middle of her vision.

A little boy. Dark hair. Dirty cheeks. Sloshing in the bathtub, water spilling over the sides.

Angry. Wanna play ball. Water sloshing.

Want. Want. Want.

Then he's playing ball, with the guys, and I am him. No water, no sloshing, just the field and the guys, and the bat in his (my?) hands.

Come. Come. Come. The song, subtle, starts as the roar of the crowd, but soon it works its way to his (my?) lips. Come. Come. Come.

He's humming it, and I'm humming it, and there's another voice, that beautiful, terrible voice, humming to him, to me. Come. Come. Come.

I feel the words to the song more than I hear them, the notes themselves bearing no resemblance to anything like language. Just sound. The sound of the crowd, the swing of the bat.

Then I'm out of the boy's body, and I see him, sitting in the tub, his eyes aimed upward, looking at something no one else can see. What's he looking at?

Eyes. I see them now: blue, blue eyes, humming.

A gray cord snakes out in beat with the song, wrapping itself around his body, and more follow, one after another after another. Like tentacles, they move through the air, catching on to his body, weaving themselves

*together until there's a net behind his body, and then they
lunge forward.*

No, not lunging. Someone pulling. Not a net. A web.

*And he hums, and she pulls, and I can almost see her
now, silver white hair cascading past smiling lips as she
hums to him, hums to him.*

*And he hums to her, and he's slipping. She pulls the
cords, pulls them, and in the next instant, he slips, out of
his body, and he's there, floating toward her, and his body's
now below, sinking. Sinking.*

And then they're gone.

I gasped audibly as I felt myself thrown out of the vision. My feet soared out from underneath me, and I
landed hard on the ground. Zo stood motionless next
to me, and I wondered how much she'd seen.

Over her shoulder, I saw the medic race into the
house, thought of the little boy they were too late to
save, and knew what I should have known all along.

"Alecca." The word escaped my lips. I'd known that
she wouldn't stop at taking half a life force. I should
have said something earlier. The thought, however il-
logical, was the first thing that leaped to mind. I'd had
my suspicions on my way here. If I'd said something,
anything . . .

"Zo?" Annabelle's voice was soft.

"We're too late," Zo said flatly. "He's gone. He
stared and hummed and hummed and stared until he
drowned."

I wished she'd swear. When Zo swore, I knew she'd be all right, but she just stood there, her mouth clenched shut.

"Alecca," I said again, not bothering to rise from the ground. It was so plain, so clear now. Adea's warnings, Zo's visions, the way the cords pulled the people right out of their bodies. I screamed at myself internally. Why hadn't it occurred to me before now that when we'd saved Amber from those cords, there was someone pulling them? That it was all tied together?

And now, a child was dead. I knew, even without Zo telling me that he was gone, that he'd slipped below the surface of the water and hadn't come back up for air.

Alecca had killed him.

Just like she was going to kill everyone at the dance. It was what I'd been afraid of all along. Marissa, Alex, and the others weren't just unconscious in the vision. They were dead.

"Don't you understand?" I asked the others, mixing up what I'd said out loud and the emotions surging through my mind. "Amber. This boy. Alecca. The dance." I couldn't seem to make a coherent sentence.

"She's doing it," Delia said, interpreting my babbling. "Whatever almost happened to Amber, whatever happened to this boy, Alecca's doing it." Delia gulped. "It's what she's going to do at the dance."

"She pulls them out of their bodies," I said softly. "I don't know how, but she does it. She pulls their . . . their . . ."

195

"Life force," Zo said dully, parroting back the term Keiri had told us earlier.

"She pulls their life force out of their body and absorbs the power." I looked down at the ground. "She eats it." I knew it was true before I said it; knew it was true when there was no way I should have known.

Annabelle spoke softly. "We should go," she said. Without a word, she put her arm around Zo. "It's almost sundown, and there's nothing we can do here."

Delia reached an arm down and helped me to my feet.

"My house is closest," Annabelle said.

Zo shook her head. "Maybe we should all just go home," she said.

Annabelle looked at her sharply. "We have things to discuss," she said.

"Do you think discussion's going to help him now?" Zo asked between clenched teeth. I wondered if she was seeing her earlier premonition through new eyes, and my stomach rolled at the thought. "Do you really think we can discuss away any of this?" Zo's voice was rougher, lower now.

"If we don't figure out how she's doing it," Annabelle said, "how are we supposed to figure out how to stop it before tomorrow night? And what if she comes after one of us beforehand? Keiri said the young have more powerful life forces, and—"

"As long as we're home, we're safe, re-mem-ber?" Zo asked, drawing out the last word and fighting off Annabelle's embrace. "Besides, what's to figure out?"

Annabelle said nothing for a moment, stunned, but then she turned toward me. "What did you see?" she asked.

Zo glared at her.

"If we're going to be walking home," Annabelle said, taking the glare as an accusation, "we may as well get the facts straight while we walk. At least that way, we'll all be free to think about it overnight."

Zo said nothing, and I knew she'd be thinking about nothing else tonight.

"Speaking of walking, maybe we should, you know, not," Delia put in hesitantly. "We'll get there faster blading, and I, personally, don't want to be out after dark when Alecca's girls-with-tattoos radar clicks and she comes to pull her freaky mojo on us, too."

Zo set her mouth in a grim line, and Annabelle stopped moving and grabbed her cousin's arm. "You are not facing off against this thing alone," she said. "And you're not going to stand outside and wait for it to come for you."

Zo didn't respond, and all I could think about was what she'd seen, what I'd seen, and the fact that I'd never met a person more confrontational or stubborn than Zo.

Annabelle bit her bottom lip and then made a decision. "It's time to go home," she said, looking Zo in the face. "You'll stay there until morning."

"It's time to go home," Zo repeated. Annabelle kept her eyes locked on her cousin's, and I knew she was putting everything she had into this mind meld.

"We shouldn't be out after dark."

"We shouldn't be out after dark."

"You can't do this alone."

"I can't do this alone."

I so didn't want to see what Zo would do if and when she ever figured out exactly what Annabelle had done to her tonight.

"So about that totally unfortunate supernatural curfew," Delia said.

Annabelle looked at Zo a second longer and then nodded.

"Let's go," she said.

Delia held her hands out to Zo's shoes, turning them into blades, and then we were off, talking as we skated downhill and toward our houses.

"Take me through this again," Annabelle told me, and because I hated myself for not saying something about my suspicions earlier, I walked her through it again.

"It's like they're in some kind of trance," I said. "She gets a hold on their minds, and then they're humming, and she's humming, and with every note of the song, she lashes out at them with this weird smoky string thing, and soon, they're wrapped up, and she pulls back on the edges of the string." I paused. I wasn't the fighter Zo was, but whatever I felt in the pit of my stomach at the thought of all this, it wasn't a feeling I recognized.

"She pulls back on the strings," Annabelle prompted.

I took a deep breath. "So she pulls back on the strings, and it catches the person up in it and pulls them out of their body."

Annabelle wrinkled her forehead, trying to get an image of what the process looked like.

I tried to explain it better. "It's like their body's empty," I said. "No one's home. Instead, there's this ghost-looking person being pulled out of the body. They're kind of transparent, but once the transparent person, the life force, I guess, is out of the person's body—"

"The soul spider," Delia said suddenly.

I turned to look at her and almost Rollerbladed straight into a tree.

"The prophecy," Delia reminded us. "The soul spider battles the end of life and death in bed." She paused. "Well, not in bed, but . . ."

"The soul spider part," Zo finished for her, not looking at any of us.

"She weaves a web," Annabelle said, working it out in her mind. "Of course. The Fates were said to spin the thread of life, to weave together the events a person would live. The spider, the weaver. It makes perfect sense."

"So she weaves a web of those tentacle thingies," I said, "and then . . ."

Soul spider.

That thing I'd seen her pull out of the person's body, it had looked just like the person, and without it, the boy had been nothing more than a shell.

It wasn't just their life force.

Annabelle spoke my thoughts, her face going even paler than usual. "She's pulling their souls out of their bodies."

"A soul sucker," Zo spit out, and the phrase sent chills up my back that nearly threw me off balance. "That's just great. I'm so glad we talked about this, because now that we know she's sucking the souls out of innocent little kids' bodies, we know exactly how to make it better before she soul-sucks the entire sophomore class." The sarcasm in her voice was almost palpable.

"We will figure something out," Annabelle said. With a long look in my direction, she veered to the left, turning toward her house and away from ours. Why did I feel as though she was going to spend all night sorting out the most logical and reasonable ways to attack a problem involving a soul-sucking fairy princess Fate?

Delia, Zo, and I skated the rest of the way home in silence. We paused in front of Delia's house as she turned our shoes back, and I noticed for the first time that her Rollerblades bore a remarkable resemblance to her high heels, with wheels added in strategic spots. It was so Delia that, had I not just seen someone's soul sucked out of his body, I might have laughed.

Even though the sun was just moments away from setting, I hung behind as Delia went into her house.

"We're going to get her," I told Zo.

She stared at me for a moment. "You can't know that," she said.

"Can't I?" I asked. Zo said nothing. "I'm descended from Guardian lines, aren't I?" I didn't let Zo answer. "I am, and I say that we're going to get her." I paused until Zo looked at me. "I promise."

Finally, she nodded. She and I didn't make promises very often, but when we did, we never broke them. Not to each other.

I turned to head into my house.

"Hey, Bay?"

"Yeah?" I looked back around.

"Thanks for coming with me," she said simply. "Into the vision. The other times I was alone, and this time . . . I was glad I wasn't, so thanks."

As Zo walked into her house, I stared after her. I hadn't felt her presence in the vision, and it hadn't really occurred to me that she'd felt mine.

Time runs thin.

The sun was setting.

Blood runs thin.

I stood there, watching, until Zo was safely inside her house, and then I ran up my driveway, just as the last trace of the sun disappeared from the horizon and night fell over the city. I reached my hand to the door.

201

Time runs thin.
Blood runs thin.
Blood recognizes blood.

My hand closed around the doorknob and twisted it. As I closed the door behind me, I let out the breath that I hadn't known I'd been holding.

"Bailey!" My mom's voice made me jump. "What in the world are you wearing?"

I followed her scandalized stare down to the "shirt" Delia had transmogrified for me that morning and groaned.

Even in the midst of a megacrisis, real life kept right on coming.

Chapter 17

I crossed my arms over my chest, waiting. I'd been here before, not that it had done me a heaping lot of good, but as
long as I was standing on the Seal, as long as I was wher-
ever it was that Adea and Valgius had been bringing me,
I was going to get some answers. They owed me that much.

"It's a delicate balance." Adea's voice was barely more
than a whisper.

Just what I'd wanted: more cryptic platitudes. In the
far corner of my mind, I added "in bed" to the end of her
statement, but forced myself to pay attention to what she
said.

"The mortal realm, our world, they exist in a careful
balance. Our power comes from your world, your lives,
and to your world, our power flows back. We weave your

lives; you sustain our powers." Adea paused, and even though her blue eyes gave no hint of it, I couldn't shake the feeling of great sadness that I felt emanating from her body.

Valgius picked up right where his lover had left off. "There has always been a balance, between life and death, mortal and Sidhe. And we, we three, were once the keepers of that balance."

"Until Alecca caught the two of you playing tonsil hockey." I clapped my hand over my mouth. I so hadn't meant to say that out loud.

Adea inclined her head slightly. "But still, there was balance. She went her way, took her power and her connection to the human race, and bided her time, trapped in a prison of her own making, under the sea."

To earth I go
From air I breathe
I command myself
Unto the sea. . . .

Alecca's spell echoed in my mind. She'd left this world willingly, and for some unfathomable reason, she'd trapped herself in the ocean.

"And because she was trapped," Valgius said quietly, "so, too, were we."

That made Alecca's plan a little more fathomable.

"Trapped by the very balance we'd sworn to protect."

I followed Adea's gaze to the Seal beneath my feet. For

204

the first time, I found myself staring at it. There was something familiar about the pattern etched into the stone surface, but I couldn't quite put my finger on it.

Without warning, the ground beneath me shook, and I could feel the Seal shifting under my feet.

"She grows stronger," Valgius said. "With each soul she takes, she grows stronger, and when she grows stronger, we grow weaker." He strained to speak. "Just one soul, but so young, so powerful, and now, our words, our knowledge, are no longer ours to give. She will take another and another, and soon, she will come for us."

"She will destroy us. She will destroy the balance."

"Tell me," I said fiercely. "Tell me how to stop her. Tell me what I can do."

Adea opened her mouth and then shut it again, her beautiful features marred by pain. "There are limits to what we can tell you," she whispered. "Limits to what we can give."

"We've given you all we can."

Adea looked sadly at the Seal beneath my feet. "The balance," she said simply, "will be destroyed."

In my mind, I saw a flash of the boy we hadn't been able to save, saw his soul ripped from his body, but this time, my legs vibrating with pressure from the Seal beneath my feet, I saw Alecca pull the boy toward her, saw her engulf him until the outline of his tiny body had been absorbed into her form.

I couldn't tear my eyes away from her face, from her blue, blue eyes. And in her eyes, I saw hunger, power, and *dozens of souls ripped from their bodies by the web she wove: the little boy; me, Annabelle, Delia, and Zo; the kids at the dance, just as Zo had foretold.*

The Seal shook beneath me, and I could see the beginnings of a crack spread through the surface like glass slowly shattering. "I know you. I have always known you."

The voice shook me to the core, my teeth chattering and my eyes tearing over. I blinked, pushing the sound of it out of my head, and when I looked down again, the Seal was whole, the crack tiny.

Nausea rolled through my body. "Adea? Valgius?" Their names left my lips before I knew I'd called for help.

No answer came as my cries echoed through the space. They were gone, and I was alone.

Time runs thin. Blood runs thin.

My heart beat with the words, and it took me a moment to realize they existed only in my memory.

Time runs thin. Blood runs thin.

I was alone.

I didn't wake up immediately, but fell instead into a restless sleep, running footraces with myself in my dreams that I could not possibly win. They were the kind of dreams that involved forgotten tests and long ago embarrassments and dogs at my heels, ready to bite.

I woke up in a pool of sweat. My hair matted to my face, I turned to look at my alarm clock. It was set to go off in another fifteen minutes. Shivering, I sat up and pulled the covers tight around my body, my mind a mix of nightmares that weren't real and nightmares that were. Without even thinking about it, I put my hand to the tattoo on my back, but there were no voices. The only sound I heard was the beating of my own heart.

"The balance," I said out loud, feeling the need to fill the silence. I tried to gather my thoughts. It looked like Alecca's plan was working. She was gaining power, and Adea and Valgius were losing it. Whatever connection I'd had with the ancient Sídhe Fates that had allowed me to hear their voices in my head was gone. I could feel it, even though I couldn't have begun to explain the logic of it all. Adea and Valgius were gone. Even awake, I was on my own.

I racked my mind, trying to remember everything I could from my dream. They'd spoken of a balance between humans and Sídhe, about being trapped. I'd seen Alecca devour the boy's soul, seen the Seal crack.

I eased my feet onto the floor of my room and groaned. My entire body felt as though someone had taken a baseball bat to it from the inside out. Trying to convince myself that a hot shower would make it all better, I stumbled my way into the bathroom.

"Well, maybe not *all* better," I mumbled under my breath, flipping on the hot spray. I had a sinking suspicion that a steamy shower couldn't fight all of the world's evils. I stepped into the steam and let the water beat against my aching skin.

I stood there until my feet ached from standing on the hard shower floor and the front half of my body was pink and numb from the spray. Moving slowly, I turned around, letting the water run down my neck, my back. As it passed over my tattoo, a shock ran up my spine, and instinctively, my hand went to cover the symbol. I turned back around, careful to shield my mark from the water and grumbling about the distinctly not-pleasant twinge I could still feel in my lower back.

"This thing should have come with a warning," I muttered. "Do not let water come into contact with tattoo. Will electrocute you immediately."

Time runs thin. Blood runs thin.

I heard my own voice inside my head, repeating the words Adea had once said to me. Flipping off the shower, I grabbed a towel and began drying off as well as I could with one hand over my tattoo.

"Sheesh," I said out loud as the sting from the water finally faded. "It wasn't like I was trying to wash it off."

The moment the words left my mouth, my heart dropped into the pit of my stomach.

Time runs thin. Blood runs thin. Tattoo. Off.

"Three days," I said, flashing back to the moment Delia had ripped open the package.

"No instructions. It just says three days. Friday to Saturday, Saturday to Sunday, Sunday to Monday. Perfect."

Her words echoed in my head.

Three days.

Perfect.

It hurt when water touched my tattoo, as if the tattoo really didn't want to be washed off. I realized about two days too late that if I'd wanted things to go back to normal, if any of us had, all we'd had to do was suffer electrocution by washing off our tattoos.

"We're idiots," I said. "All of us." We'd gotten our powers when we'd put on temporary tattoos. Key word: *temporary*. Keiri had said that the tattoos were written in Sídhe blood; that the powers came to us through that blood.

Temporary tattoos. Temporary powers.

It had been there on the package the whole time. Three days. Three days before the blood ran thin.

Three days that ended today, or more specifically, tonight during the dance. Even if we could somehow manage to get the dance called off (that was the best idea I'd managed to come up with in the shower), that didn't buy us any more time to stop Alecca. After tonight, we wouldn't have any powers. We wouldn't be able to fight her.

I rushed for my bedroom, bursting with the knowledge and ready to race across the street to get Delia and Zo, when I realized that I was still wearing nothing but a towel and a tattoo I so didn't want anyone to see.

Haphazardly throwing on clothes, I assembled an outfit that I knew would make Delia lock me in fashion prison and severely tempt her to destroy the key, but given the current state of affairs, that really wasn't one of my priorities.

I ran down the steps, tripped over the last one, and promptly fell flat on my face.

And I was supposed to save the entire school. Poor school.

"Slow down, honey. No need to hurry. You won't miss the bus. In fact, you actually have time for breakfast this morning."

"Mom, I really don't have time," I said, clamoring to my feet. "I really need to talk to Zo, and—"

She cut me off with a single raise of her left eyebrow. The left eyebrow raise was never a good thing, and it usually ended up with her in lecture mode or me grounded. "You spent all of yesterday with Zo," my mother said. "You saw plenty of her and Delia and Annabelle this weekend. They spent Friday night over here, and we barely saw anything of you on Saturday, and on Sunday you came home so tired you just collapsed into bed and barely touched your dinner."

To my mother, that was a cardinal sin.

"You've spent more time with them in the past three days than you have with your family in weeks, so don't tell me that you don't have time to sit down and eat breakfast because you have to rush over to Zo's." My mom fixed me to the spot where I stood with another look, raising her eyebrow even higher and daring me to argue. "There's nothing so important that you can't wait another fifteen minutes to tell her."

The lives of hundreds are at stake, I pictured myself saying, because an evil fairy princess who doubles as one of the three Fates is sucking out the souls of innocent people, and my friends and I have been imbued with the powers to stop her, but we only have the powers for like another twelve hours, and I really need to talk to them about what we can do to save the balance of the worlds and everyone at my high school, including Alex Atkins, the bane of my existence.

I opened my mouth and then shut it again. There was no world in which me telling my mother that could end well. Biting my bottom lip to make sure I didn't accidentally blurt it all out, I followed her grudgingly back to the kitchen, where she loaded my plate full of bacon, eggs, and still-hot biscuits.

"So, what did you want to talk to Zo about?"

I took a big bite of biscuit to refrain from answering the question. The only good thing about talking around the breakfast table was that chewing each bite twenty-three times made for a wonderful stalling technique.

"Just stuff," I answered vaguely. My mom leaned in, and I could sense a barrage of questions coming on. "Dance stuff," I said. That much at least was true. "I . . . uh . . . think Delia might have a date."

I sent a silent apology to Delia, because I knew my mom would grill her the next time they spoke, but it was the first thing I'd been able to come up with, and as I said it, I realized it was probably true. Delia Cameron wasn't the type to go to any dance without a date, not even the dance of doom.

"Oh really," my mom said, fascinated. "But she hasn't told you guys about it yet?"

I shook my head. Usually Delia was an open book when it came to guys and dating. Anyone within a ten-yard radius knew more than they wanted to about her dating life, but the past few days hadn't given us much girl-talk time.

Ten minutes and a bunch of vague references to Delia and boys later, I was out of my kitchen just in time to see the school bus pulling up in front of my house. Zo and Delia were already climbing on, and I had to jog in order to catch up to them before the bus driver shut the door and drove off without me.

We made our way to the back of the bus, where Annabelle always saved us seats.

"I need to talk to you guys." I didn't bother with small talk.

"So talk." Zo still wasn't in an exactly charming mood.

Annabelle glanced around, and then leaned over to whisper something to the seventh graders sitting next to us.

"Hey, man, let's sit up front," one of them said.

"Yeah," his friend agreed. "I want to sit in the front of the bus."

I shot Annabelle a grateful look and began. "We're in way, way over our heads."

"You think?" Delia asked. The sweet, pretty-girl tone in her voice almost masked the sarcasm.

"I agree with Bailey," Annabelle said. "I was thinking last night, and—"

I interrupted Annabelle, the knowledge that our time was running out building up inside me until I had to blurt it out. "Three days," I said. The others stared at me, their expressions ranging from thoughtful to looking at me as if I was speaking Latin. "On the tattoo package," I continued, "it said three days. That's how long our powers last." I looked at each one of them in turn. "That's how long we have to beat this thing."

"We put them on to last through the dance," Delia said automatically, and then she realized what she'd just said. "And the dance is tonight."

"Tonight," Zo said, and even though there was no emotion in her voice, I knew that she wasn't just thinking about our tattoos. She was thinking about what she'd seen, seeing it again through new eyes.

"Time runs thin." I forced myself to repeat the words I'd heard so many times. "I had another dream last night. Adea and Valgius can't help us anymore," I said. "There's some kind of balance thingy, and since this *thing* is becoming more powerful, they've gotten weaker, and now I can't even hear them in my head anymore."

"What else do you remember?" Annabelle immediately started grilling me. She could have given my mom lessons in probing-question technique—everything I'd managed to piece together came tumbling out of my mouth.

"So basically," Zo said when we were finished, "we're screwed."

"That would be the gist of it, yeah," I said.

"We wouldn't have been given these powers if we didn't stand a chance at stopping her," Annabelle said in a way that almost made me believe her. "I thought about it, and I think we may be able to trap her somehow, *before* the dance." Annabelle wrinkled her forehead. "From what Bailey said about the balance, maybe we should come up with a plan that would swing the balance back in the other direction and sap Alecca of her power."

"And how do you propose we do that?" Zo asked.

"Carefully," Annabelle said immediately.

And with charts, I added silently, but for the first time since this whole thing had started, charts and research seemed to be the farthest thing from Annabelle's mind. Now she was all about strategy.

"We each have our gifts," she said. "We've been given them for a reason. They must work together somehow. Maybe if I can enter Alecca's mind, Bailey can enshroud her in some kind of ring of fire. Zo, you could divine for her weakness, a physical weak spot, and then Delia could transmogrify something to attack that spot."

That was so a better course of action than I'd managed to come up with.

"What we need is to plan the attack down to the most minute detail," Annabelle said.

"Oh joy." Zo was more of a fighter than a planner.

Annabelle ignored her cousin. "Unfortunately," she continued, "we have two pretty big problems."

214

Problems. Like we didn't have enough of those already.

"The first problem is that in order to fight Alecca, we need to find her," Annabelle said. "That would be Zo's department. We can't really plan an attack if we have no idea where it's going to take place."

"And the second problem?" I asked, knowing this one was going to be a doozy.

"Well," Annabelle said, "today's Mabon."

I glanced at Delia and Zo and saw that the significance of that statement wasn't ringing any bells with them, either.

"The fall equinox," Annabelle reminded us. "The day and night are equally long." Annabelle looked at me. "If what you said about Adea and Valgius not being able to help you is true, it supports my theory." Annabelle said the word "theory" almost apologetically, as if she knew she was starting to sound too academic for her own good. "When you first told us about the 'unfortunate supernatural curfew,' you said that Adea warned you that daylight would shield us so long as light was in the majority."

Annabelle took a deep breath. "Before Mabon," she said, "the day is longer than the night. After Mabon, the night is longer than the day."

"In other words," Zo finished up for her cousin, "the light is no longer in the majority."

"And Adea and Valgius aren't blocking her anymore," I said, knowing it was true. "They just can't."

"So, let me get this straight," Delia said. "Problem one is that we don't know if we'll be able to find her before the dance?" Annabelle nodded. "And problem two," Delia continued, pausing only for a moment, "is that we're afraid she'll find us."

I turned to Zo and the question flew off my lips before it had fully formed in my mind. "In your vision," I said, "of the dance . . . were we there?"

Zo didn't say anything, and I knew the answer was no.

The bus pulled to a stop at the high school, and I noticed for the first time that somehow, in the midst of all our strategy talk, Delia had managed to transmogrify the bus into a limo. Not quite covert, but we didn't exactly have time to worry about being covert anymore.

"So what do we do?" I asked, hoping Annabelle had a nice and nifty logical answer.

For a moment, there was silence.

"We get out of the limo," Delia said, "and then we worry about the rest."

We stepped out of the car, and I couldn't help but glance around the schoolyard. A couple of jocks were standing on top of a picnic table; that guy with the thick glasses was duct-taped to a tree. Marissa Baker was probably hidden away in the newspaper room, writing another article that no one cared about, and Alex . . .

Alex had her arms draped over Kane's shoulders.

I thought of my dream, of the way he'd looked at

216

me and the way I'd felt inside, and then I looked back at Alex as she mesmerized every male in the near vicinity with a bouncy-boob laugh that was so obvious it made Delia look like the queen of subtle.

"And we're supposed to save *that*," Annabelle said, lifting the thought from my mind.

Murderous fairy-Fates aside, life was so not fair.

Chapter 18

As I sat in my math class, listening to my teacher drone on about the law of sines, I felt like a walking time bomb. With every sound in the room, every pencil moving across a page, every note passed, every whisper, I jumped in my seat, half-expecting to see a gray tentacle come out of nowhere to devour the entire class. Everywhere I looked, I saw Alecca: saw her red lips, saw her silver blond hair, saw her dead, blue eyes. I saw her ripping their souls out of their bodies and the red lips swallowing them whole. What if she decided not to wait for the dance? What if she knew Zo had seen it and decided to strike early? What if there was nothing I could do about it?

Honestly, that last question didn't seem like much of a what-if.

"Excuse me, Mr. Andrews." An office aide poked her head into the room, and I could feel the entire class sigh with relief for any break from the doldrums of basic trig. If they only knew. "The office needs to see Bailey Morgan."

I grabbed my things, then hesitated before following the aide out of the room. Luring me to my death through the school's administration didn't seem like Alecca's style, but even so, I imagined her voice taunting me as I walked.

You won't win. You can't.

That's what she would say to me if she had the chance. I half-wondered if she *was* saying it to me, if she was speaking to me the way Adea and Valgius had before Alecca killed the boy. Biting my bottom lip so hard it ached, I opened the door to the office.

"Ah, yes, Ms. Morgan," the principal said the moment he saw me. "You're to report to the gym. The dance committee is finishing up a few things and they need your help."

I couldn't decide if he was speaking English or not. The dance committee? My help? A world of yeah right.

"The dance committee?" I repeated skeptically.

The principal gave me a look. "Yes," he said impatiently. "Annabelle Porter distinctly said that your assistance was needed."

I tried not to look conspicuous and failed miserably. "Oh yeah," I said, doing my best to cover up the sketchy expression I knew I was sporting. "*That* committee."

219

"Took you long enough," Zo said when I stepped into the gym three minutes later.

"This is so much better than class," Delia said. She sighed. "I'm really going to miss these powers." She changed subjects without so much as skipping a beat. "These are great decorations."

It was just like Delia to critique the decorations in the middle of what could only be described as an epic battle we were destined to lose.

Not wanting to look at Annabelle, who I knew could hear my pessimistic thoughts as well as I could, I looked around. The actual dance committee had already decked the gym out with shiny, silver streamers, dark purple accent pieces, and a veritable ton of helium balloons, which would probably sink midway to the floor by the time the dance actually started.

I could practically hear the music in my head, could see myself dancing with Kane.

"Your hair . . ."

No time to daydream, I reminded myself. Must concentrate on evil fairy. Why was it that whenever I thought of Kane, nothing else seemed to matter?

"Can we return to the matter at hand?" Annabelle said. "If we want to destroy her, we must consider the nature of our enemy." Annabelle sounded so official that I felt an odd urge to salute her. "We know that she is Sídhe and that, as such, she commands some Sídhe powers."

"Like sucking souls out of people?" Zo suggested drily.

A little boy dreaming about Little League, dead in the bathtub.

"Our powers are Sídhe powers," Annabelle said, and her soft, authoritative voice broke me from the mental image. "They come from the blood in the tattoos. I think it makes sense to assume that Alecca might be armed with some of the same powers." Moving quickly, Annabelle presented us with a sheet of paper.

"Our symbols?" I asked.

"Yes," Annabelle said. "Like Lionel told us, separately they translate roughly to fire, knowledge, future, and change." Annabelle flipped the paper over and gestured to the symbols drawn on the back. "And here we have two of the combined symbols," she said. "Life and death." She nodded to a final drawing. "And the combination of the combinations, balance."

Delia messed with one of her nails as Annabelle prattled on.

"Balance is composed of life and death. Life, as you can see, is composed of fire and knowledge, and death of future and change." Annabelle paused. "If you think about it, it makes sense." She looked down. "Death is in the future for us all, and it is a change."

"But you think it might mean something more?" Delia asked.

"It's just a hypothesis," Annabelle said, "but I think

that maybe death and life refer in fact to Sister Death and Sister Life." She paused. "To Alecca and Adea," she clarified. Annabelle said their names so easily that I couldn't help but think that she didn't know them, didn't fully realize what was at stake.

How could she? She hadn't seen what Zo and I had seen the night before. She'd never seen Alecca.

"So," Annabelle continued on with her theory, seemingly unaware of my thoughts, "maybe Adea and Alecca have the powers encompassed by their symbols. For death, premonition and transmogrification; for life, pyrokinesis and mind control."

"Can we just call her Death instead of Alecca?" I found myself asking. "It fits a lot better."

"What's the point of this?" Zo asked impatiently.

"The point is that we can't forget that our enemy is an unknown, and that we have to plan to fight against whatever powers she may possess." Annabelle took a deep breath. "We need to cement our plan of action before Alecca finds us."

"Wouldn't it be better if she found us?" Zo asked. "I mean, if we find her, we're on her turf, but if she finds us"—Zo made a sardonic gesture toward the silver streamers—"if she finds us here, we have more control."

"Are you suggesting we just stay in one place until she finds us?" Annabelle asked, her voice echoing in the nearly empty gym.

"Sure," Zo said.

"Problem," I said. "What if she doesn't find us until later?" I looked down at my feet. "What if she finds us after we've lost our powers?" I paused. "Or what if she finds the others first?"

I didn't need to elaborate for them to know I was referring to the people from Zo's vision.

"Okay, new plan," Zo said immediately. "We find her."

"Do you have a scrying crystal with you?" Annabelle asked Zo. Zo nodded and lifted Keiri's crystal out of her pocket.

"Never go anywhere without it," Zo said.

"Mark the calendar," Delia said automatically. "Zo is accessorized."

Zo made a face at Delia. "Map?" she asked.

"Map of what?" Annabelle's question was, of course, the epitome of logic. "We don't even know for sure that she's in this world."

"If I don't have a map, what am I supposed to scry off of?" Zo demanded.

"Close your eyes." The direction was out of my mouth before I knew I'd given it. "Let images come to you. See the town, the world. See whatever image comes to your mind, and just really look at it."

As I spoke, my voice took on an almost hypnotic tone, and Zo closed her eyes. The crystal in her hand swung in circles, gently at first and then erratically, darting left and right, front and back at an uneven pace.

223

"The ocean," Zo said, her voice labored and her body tense. "The hotel. Another place . . . I can't . . . it's almost there, but . . ."

The crystal flew out of her hand and shattered against the opposite wall.

The hairs on the back of my neck stood up as I looked around. Except for us and the balloons, the gym was empty.

"I'm guessing that Death doesn't really like being scried for." Delia's voice was shaky as she tucked a strand of chestnut-colored hair behind her ear.

"I almost had it," Zo bit out, opening her eyes. "I could see where she'd been. I could feel where she was, but when it came to actually knowing the answer, actually finding her, I was . . ."

"Blocked?" Annabelle suggested.

Zo nodded, her face still dark. "Yeah."

"Sídhe-blocked," I said, remembering the term Keiri had used. "Like my dreams and Annabelle's thoughts when she's wearing the magic barrette."

I felt ridiculous for even using the phrase "magic barrette."

"You think this is a magic necklace?" Delia asked, fingering the black metal choker she wore around her neck. "I got it at the same booth where you got the tattoos and Annabelle got her barrette."

"Does it do anything?" I asked lamely.

"Other than accentuate my chest, not really," Delia

replied, "but the saleswoman said it was retro and cutting, and I have to agree."

Zo snorted, but the next second, she was diving for her backpack.

"What?" the rest of us asked at once.

Zo unzipped the front pocket and took out a small white bag. Gingerly, she opened it and took something into her hands. Opening her fist, she let the dark purple crystal swing down, the nearly invisible cord held in between her middle finger and her thumb.

"Another scrying crystal," Zo explained. "I almost forgot I had it, but I bought it at the mall when you guys were buying your"—Zo physically had to force herself to say the word—"accessories."

"If my barrette and the tattoos are magicked," Annabelle said evenly, "your crystal may well be also."

Zo nodded, and closed her eyes. The crystal moved, and soon it was swinging counterclockwise in a triangular motion. It whistled through the air, lightly, purposefully, and I found myself watching it.

"She's near," Zo said softly. "Not in our world, but in another that runs parallel. She's watching. She's near."

I watched the crystal dance on the end of the string, and slowly, the sound of Zo's voice faded from my ears. I could feel myself being pulled from reality, and after a moment, all I saw was the crystal, and all I heard was the beating of my own heart, and then there was nothing.

"I've been waiting for you." Gently, he pulled me toward him. "Shall we dance?"

Part of me knew it was a dream, knew it couldn't be real, but I didn't care. Here, in this place, he wasn't listening to Alex, wasn't watching her laugh. Her arms weren't around him; his were around me.

The lights dimmed as his arms encircled my waist, and I rested my head on his shoulders. The music began playing, and we swayed to it.

"Your hair looks like moonlight."

My heart pounded viciously against the inside of my rib cage, and I could feel his beating next to mine. His hands played along my arms until his fingertips touched mine. My fingers tingled with his touch, and after a moment, he brought his hands to my cheeks.

"You're beautiful."

"No," I said, staring back into his eyes. "You are."

He laughed then. "You surprise me," he said. "Everything about you surprises me."

I could feel his breath on my face, and it made my skin heat up.

"Your eyes surprise me every time I look into them and they're looking back at me." He brought his hands gently to the side of my face. "Your mouth surprises me, because you always seem to smile more with one half than with the other, like part of you knows a funny secret that none of the rest of us, not even your other half, can guess."

He brushed a finger over my lips, and I sucked in a breath. This was so right. It all felt so right.

"You surprise me, Bailey Morgan," he said. We swayed to the music, and the tune filled my head. This was so right, and I wanted it with all of my being. Wanted him.

"Do you want me?" he asked me softly. He brought his lips to mine, holding back from kissing me by just a fraction of an inch. "Because I want you."

I wanted him. Wanted him.

I moved forward, caught up in the moment and the music and his lips and mine. "I've wanted this for so long," I murmured.

Want. Want. Want.

"I know." He moved his lips toward mine, closing the gap between them in what seemed like slow motion. "I've always known you."

It was perfect, and as his lips closed over mine, I lost track of everything except for the kiss, and the music swelled around me.

Come. Come. Come.

It was so warm, so right, that for a moment, I wanted to stay there, with him, forever, and then his words caught up with me.

I know you. I've always known you.

I pulled away from him and for the first time realized that even as we kissed, he was humming. I was humming. There was no music playing. We were dancing to the sound of our own humming.

227

Come. Come. Come.

I know you. I've always known you.

What had Keiri said about the trio? "They were to know human life, to know humans, and through their knowledge, the power inherent in all life was to return to the Sídhe."

"I know you. I've always known you. Don't you want me, Bailey?" Kane asked, but looking at him, I knew that they weren't Kane's words, that he wasn't real. "Isn't this what you wanted?"

Want. Want . . .

I shook my head, taking a step back.

"I want you." His voice was soft and low, and so, so sweet.

"Stop it," I said, pushing him away. "Just stop it."

This wasn't real. None of this was real. Biting back tears, I pushed the sound of the song out of my head. "Stop it."

"Bailey, I don't understand." Kane looked at me, longing and hurt on his face, and, oh, I wanted him. Wanted him, but it wasn't him.

None of this was real.

"This is what you want, what you've always wanted," the creature with Kane's face, his voice, said, and I understood why Alecca would choose a high school dance for her hunting grounds. Somehow, she preyed on desires, and everyone in high school wanted something. Even me.

My eyes stung with tears. Oh, I wanted it even now, but

228

it wasn't real. "No!" *I found myself yelling.* "I don't want it. I don't want any of it, not from you. Not ever."

"Bailey—"

"Stop saying my name. Stop using his voice." *A single tear streamed down my face, and as it fell off my cheek and onto the floor below, I felt the music's hold on me tremble.* "I don't want it, Alecca."

The moment the name left my lips, the world around me crumbled into a different scene. I wasn't standing in the gym, and Kane wasn't standing with me. There were no streamers or balloons. I wasn't beautiful.

"Bailey. OMG, Bailey. We thought you were a goner."

I turned at the sound of Delia's voice.

"Your eyes glazed over, Bay, and you just kept staring, and when you started humming . . ." Zo trailed off and stuffed her hands in her pockets.

"You couldn't hear us." Annabelle's voice was soft as she surveyed our surroundings. "One minute you were there, and the next you were gone."

"Like Amber." Zo's voice was hard. "Like the boy."

"I . . ." How was I supposed to explain what had happened? All I knew was that my daydream had been something far more serious and that if I'd held on to Kane's kiss, if I'd let myself want it all for a moment longer, the desire would have swallowed me whole.

"Where are we?" Zo changed the subject. I could have hugged her for it.

229

I looked around. "We're standing on the Seal," I said softly. I'd stood here before, been here before in my dreams, but now I wasn't dreaming, and I wasn't alone.

As it turned out, neither were we.

"Such a pity. I do detest bloodshed."

I whirled around to face the speaker, but before I could, I felt an invisible force lash out at me, and like a whip of fire across my entire body, it threw me to the floor.

"Okay, fairy," Zo said evenly. "Now it's on."

Chapter 19

"Big words from such a small mortal." Alecca's voice was painfully sweet. "Would you like to be bigger, little one?" Alecca smiled an awful smile, her bloodred lips curving beautifully on her ivory face. "No . . . I know what you want, Zoe-Claire."

We knew her name, and she knew ours. I had a feeling that whatever advantage calling her by name had won me, it was over now. We were on even footing, and on her turf.

"You want your mother," Alecca said, and her words hit me hard. Looking over, I knew they hit Zo harder. "You want her to see you and your dad, to see that you don't need her, but sweetling, you do, and I think you know that, don't you?"

"Don't talk about her mother," Annabelle said through clenched teeth.

"Do you think I lie, Annabelle? Yes, I know your name, too, child. I know you all. I know what you feel. I know what you think. I know what you want, and I can give it to you." She took a step forward. I tried to clamber to my feet, but found myself pushed back down by the force of Alecca's gaze.

"Do you know what I'm thinking now?" Annabelle asked, never backing down. "You don't."

Alecca said nothing, but I couldn't help but glance at the barrette in Annabelle's hair.

I caught Annabelle's gaze out of the corner of my eye, and she nodded slightly. Trying my best to remember the tentative plan of attack she'd outlined earlier, I threw my entire self into creating flame.

My skin itched with the burning sensation in my blood, as emotion coursed through my body. She'd taken so much. She'd ripped the soul from the body of a child. She'd killed him, and she planned to kill more. She'd do anything to get her revenge. She'd taken Kane from me, from that sacred crush place in the back of my mind and the front of my heart.

She was insulting my friends.

The heat built up inside my body. It pumped through my veins and fought against my skin.

I looked at Alecca standing there with her blue eyes and rose red grin, and I stopped holding the power back. I let every emotion, every worry, every bit of heat in my body flow from my hands, and fire leaped from my palm to her body.

The floor in front of her burst into flame, and I could feel the earth shifting beneath me, the Seal splintering as the ground shuddered.

"Zo, weakness," Annabelle called out. "Quickly."

Zo closed her eyes, her hand still clenched over the crystal she'd used to divine Alecca's presence.

"Weakness is mortal," Alecca said, stepping through the flames. "I am not."

"Whatever her weakness is," Zo hissed under her breath, "Bailey's standing on it."

The Seal.

My concentration wavered, and so did the fire. I bit my bottom lip and sent another wave of heat toward Alecca as she approached me and the Seal. With a casual flick of her hand, she sent a stream of brilliant blue-green flame flying right back at me.

"What is the expression you mortals use?" she asked, her red lips curving into a smirk. "Fighting fire with fire?"

Burning heat surrounded me, separating me from my friends with a wall of angry blood green flames.

Pyrokinesis. She had pyrokinesis? So much for Annabelle's theory.

"I could have given you your heart's desire, could have given you all you've ever wanted." Alecca stepped through the fire. "It was beautiful, what I offered you. And what did I ask in return?" She shrugged. "Your life, your soul, your power: such a small price for a moment of true happiness."

I snorted, because as long as I was snorting, I wasn't, technically, quaking in my boots. "That's your master plan?" I asked. "Give people what they think they want and while they're all wrapped up in it, you take their souls?"

"I weave," Alecca said simply. "We are not so different, you and I. I do what I was born to do." Her eyes flashed. "I weave your lives, and if you get caught in a web of desires, a web of hopes and dreams and all else you mortals coddle in your heart of hearts . . ." She sneered at this last expression. "Is it truly my fault for spinning the web? Or is it yours, for giving it to me to spin?"

Her question lay heavy with me. She'd been targeting me all along. She knew what the others wanted. She knew that Zo wanted her mother, and yet, she'd targeted me. Why?

"Because, little one, blood is drawn to blood. Like recognizes like." She paused. "You're Sídhe enough to want deeply, human enough to die."

I felt pressure on my neck, an invisible hand closing over my throat and pushing me back and toward the unberable heat of the fire.

"I wanted once," she said, advancing on me even as she forced me into the flame. "Wanted deeply, wanted badly, and because of you, because I know humans, I thought I loved."

234

So she *had* been in love with Valgius, I thought.

The vise around my neck tightened and I choked.

"I was wrong."

No air. I couldn't breathe, and the heat of the blue-green fire played with my skin, tearing at it with scorching claws. I would have cried out, but there was no air, no voice with which for me to cry.

"Fruit punch!"

As if from a great distance, I heard Delia's cry, and the flame around me dissolved into a massive wave of fruity red liquid. For a moment, Alecca was distracted enough that her mental hold on my throat relaxed, and desperately, I breathed in, swallowing the air and choking in desperation to breathe it all in at once.

Alecca frowned the way people frown when they've discovered a speck on their carpet. She turned a mildly annoyed look on Delia.

Delia stepped forward, no trace of fear on her face. "You think you're bad?" Delia asked her. "I've seen worse. I'm on the cheerleading squad; I know what *real* evil looks like."

"If you mess with Bailey," Zo said, her voice quiet and deadly, "you mess with us all."

Alecca laughed merrily. "How precious," she said. "You think you can hurt me, little one? Will you throw your crystal at me? It would take something far more ancient and far more powerful than that trinket to hurt me."

My mind raced. With the Seal broken, she wasn't

235

invincible. There had to be some way, some weakness we could attack.

I stumbled to my feet, and Alecca knocked me off the Seal and across the room with a careless gesture. My head made a sickening thunking sound as it hit the floor, and pain ripped across my skull like dull, aching fire. I reached my hand to the back of my head, and when I brought it back, it was coated in blood.

The world blurred in front of me, but I fought the dizziness and the unforgiving throb in my head.

Alecca shook her head. "I do detest bloodshed," she said for the second time. "What a pity."

Zo, furious and fearless, looked about five seconds away from telling Alecca exactly what she could do with her pity. There she was, more or less powerless, and yet pyrokinetic me was the one lying on the floor, bleeding.

Alecca stepped toward me.

Hoping Annabelle would catch my thought, I put all my concentration into the words: *Keep her on the Seal.*

Annabelle nodded. "There are things that can hurt you," Annabelle said. "Ancient things. Things of power that were made to stop one such as you."

Alecca stopped advancing on me and turned toward Annabelle. "There are no others like me," she said. "I alone have lived with you. I alone have felt the power of the human soul. I, and I alone."

"Egotistical much?" Delia had Alecca whirling around.

"Understatement of the year," Zo muttered. "I and I alone," she mimicked.

Fury creased Alecca's otherwise flawless face and she turned her wrath on Zo, who stood her ground, never flinching, never moving back.

Zo. She should have been afraid. I wanted to get up, to save her, but I couldn't. Luckily, Delia Cameron was on the job.

"Is that your natural hair color?" Delia asked, drawing Alecca's attention. "Because I have to tell you, I think it's a bit overdone. No subtlety." As Delia talked, she pulled her choker off her neck. Alecca didn't notice, but since I knew for a fact that Delia didn't part with accessories unless under major duress, the movement caught my eye.

In a single movement, Delia tossed the necklace to Zo, who looked at it as if it was a squashed slug.

Annabelle narrowed her eyes at Delia, and then comprehension hit.

"Zo," she said. "Throw it."

Zo moved lightning fast, flicking the choker directly at Alecca, who turned to see it a moment too late. As if pulled by an invisible force, the choker latched around her throat. Alecca clawed at it, but the choker merely tightened until it cut into her neck. A thin line of blue-green blood welled to the surface of her white skin.

"Something more ancient than this, huh?" Zo asked, holding up her crystal. Alecca stood, frozen to the Seal, her fingers madly tearing at the choker. "I'm guessing that's a little more ancient."

Delia stepped forward. "It's ancient," she said. "In fact, I'd say it was retro and *cutting*, wouldn't you, guys?"

Alecca's blood dripped onto the Seal, and it exploded, shattering down the center. The next instant, it collapsed in on itself. The ground split beneath the Seal, and the growing crevice engulfed Alecca. Before I could so much as blink, she was gone.

Cautiously, Annabelle tiptoed over to look down at the hole in the ground that had opened beneath the Seal. "She's gone."

My head swam with her words.

"Bay, are you okay?" Zo asked, and in an instant, all of them were by my side. "It's gonna be okay, Bailey. It's over. You're going to be fine."

I thought of Adea and Valgius, thought of the balance the Seal protected, thought of our world and theirs, and I shook my head, my whole body ringing with the motion of it. "It's not over," I said, pulling myself along the ground toward the Seal.

It was then that I realized why it looked so familiar. "Our symbols," I said. "The Seal."

"It's our tattoos," Delia breathed, seeing the same thing I did.

"That's what you get when you superimpose all of the symbols," Zo said.

"Balance." Annabelle provided the translation I already knew, and knowledge seeped over me.

"I have to close it." It was what I'd been born to do.

"Whatever needs to be done, we're in it together," Zo said, and she pulled me to my feet. "Lean on me."

In the next instant, Delia was on my other side.

"Take her to the Seal," Annabelle said softly, lifting the desire from my mind.

"But, Bailey, it's broken, and no offense, but you've got to be crazy to want to step on that thing," Delia said. "It just ate Alecca."

"Please," I said. Together, the three of us walked to the Seal, and Annabelle followed, her hand on Zo's shoulder.

To fight, to live
We two of three bestow this gift
To see, to feel
To stand upon the ancient Seal

The words came to me, ghosts of things I'd heard Adea and Valgius say when we'd first applied the tattoos.

"We're standing here," I said tiredly, my head spinning. "We're standing upon the ancient Seal. Now what?"

"Bailey, you're bleeding!" Delia's voice was horrified.

That wasn't exactly news to me, but as I heard her words, blood dripped off the back of my head and onto the Seal below me. It quaked beneath my feet, but I stood firm.

It's in the blood. Things of power always are.

And then, I knew.

"My blood." I whispered the words, my voice hoarse.

Adea and Valgius had given us their blood, and now I was giving the Seal mine.

"To fight, to live
you two of three bestowed this gift . . ."

I altered the words of the original spell to make it my own. After a moment, Annabelle picked up on my thoughts, and her voice joined in with mine.

"We see, we feel
We stand upon the ancient Seal . . ."

When Zo and Delia joined in, I knew that Annabelle was somehow silently feeding them the words.

"From earth she came
from air she breathed . . ."

The words to the spell were changing more now, but instinctively, I knew what to say, and with every word I spoke, the others echoed me.

"From deep within her hatred seethed
Fires burned
Desires freed
And as we will . . ."

I felt Zo's grip on my side tighten as we spoke the final words: "So mote it be."

The words sounded foreign to my ears but felt right on my lips, and as we spoke them, holding on to each other as if we would never let go, the earth beneath us shuddered, and the Seal fell gently back into place, piecing itself together moment by moment, until it was whole.

Rays of light burst from the stone markings, flooding us with warmth, and I could feel my head healing itself. In my last conscious moment, I lifted my hand to touch the back of my head, then brought my fingers to my eyes.

My hand was covered in blood. Blue-green blood.

Chapter 20

I struggled to open my eyes.

"Rest, child." The voice was soothing, but I recognized the power in it, the ancientness of it, and I struggled to open my eyes. If I'd learned anything in the past three days, it was that voices like that weren't to be trusted.

The first thing I saw when I opened my eyes was the ocean. It was all around me. I yelped when I discovered it was beneath me. I was sitting on the ocean's surface.

"You need not fear harm here." The rhyme was pleasant, as was the voice that spoke it. It was a familiar voice. I turned slowly toward the speaker, bracing myself against the water beneath me.

"You," I said, and it came out like an accusation.

The woman smiled. "Yes," she said. "Me."

I'd seen her blue eyes before, when she'd sold us the tattoos. "We went back," I said, "to find you, to ask you about our powers, but the sign on the booth said that it was closed in preparation for Mabon."

"A hint," the woman said. "As much of one as I could give you to draw your attention to the equinox and the events it would bring."

"And the booth?" I asked.

"For you and you alone," the woman said.

I should have known from the blue eyes, and for that matter, it should have occurred to me that they didn't typically sell destiny-altering magical accessories at the mall. "You knew we'd be there?"

"I knew the time was coming," she said. "Your Alecca imprisoned herself in my waters millennia ago. I knew the time for her release was nigh."

"So you gave us the tattoos?" I asked.

"Those were not of my doing," the woman said.

"Adea and Valgius." I'd thought as much.

The woman nodded. "It took others among the Sídhe much longer to realize that the worlds had been breached, that the trio had been broken, but from the moment she stepped foot in my waters, I knew. Her anger, her power seeped into the water like toxin, and I sought out the other young ones to offer what help I could."

I stared at her for a moment. Had she just referred to Adea and Valgius as young ones?

"To me, they are young," the woman said. "My tie to your world and your people predates the necessity of their birth."

"Oh." There didn't seem to be an appropriate response to that.

"The two who remained with the Seal were in a horrible position," the woman said. "They could not leave, and they could not indefinitely stay. To venture forth from the Seal would surely rip it apart and sever the power of the Sídhe and perhaps all mortal life, but to stay meant to offset the balance: two in the Otherworld, one in this."

"You're darned if you do, you're darned if you don't." I couldn't believe I'd just said that. I might as well have said "nifty" and "gee whiz" while I was at it.

"Something like that," the woman agreed, "and so, with my help, they did what they could to prevent the collapse of the Seal. They sent their blood and the blood of the other Sister into the world, carrying with it the powers they held most dear, so that when the battle came, those who would fight it would be armed."

"Us." That part was easy enough to follow. "They gave you the blood, and you made the tattoos," I said. "The symbols, that was you?"

The woman smiled. "Another hint."

I waited, sensing there was more to this story.

"They also sent with me something of greater value, and there is little the Sídhe value more than Sídhe blood." She paused. "They sent with me the child Adea carried in

244

her womb, the child born from their love. I took the blood and the child to the place where they would do the balance the most good." She looked at me. "This world."

Wow. A fairy/Fate love child. Zo had been right all along. This whole thing was just a giant interdimensional soap opera.

"Their hope, my hope was that the child would live among humans, would have her own children and their children after that for years and years, so that when Alecca broke free, when the power shifted toward her side of the imbalance, there would be a child on this side who could fight her." The woman looked at me. "A child who would be drawn to the blood they'd given me, a child worthy of the fight."

She stopped speaking, waiting for me to say what was becoming more and more clear. "Me?" I squeaked.

I'd just gotten used to the idea that my ancestors had been blessed by the Sídhe, and now she was telling me that my ancestors were Sídhe?

"You," the woman said. "You chose the tattoos; they chose you. I guided your friends toward those items I thought could best protect them and serve them. This was never meant to be a mortal fight, so I gave them all that I could."

I asked a question that had been bothering me for days. "Did I find the tattoos because Alecca was getting ready to rise, or did Alecca rise because I found the tattoos?"

"Good question, child. Applying the blood awakened

the power that slumbered in you, the power that had slumbered in this world for thousands of your generations, and this power shifted the balance toward this side of the Seal."

"And Alecca woke up."

"You could say that." The woman looked at me, lifting the rest of the questions easily from my mind. "The necklace your friend wore was forged from this sea long before Alecca spun her first human life. It is raw, pure, and contains a great deal of silver, which is poisonous to the younger ones of our kind."

"And the blood?" I swallowed hard. "Her blood, I mean, and then my blood . . ." I wasn't making much sense, but it didn't matter.

"She took herself from the Seal long ago, and by taking a human soul, she weakened it until it cracked. Her blood, when shed upon the Seal, atoned for the imbalance, and the Seal itself consumed her." She smiled softly. "Your blood righted things, in more ways than one. You were Sídhe enough to fight her, Bailey, and human enough to win. You are a balance unto yourself: mortal and fairy, human and Sídhe." She paused. "You invoked the Seal, and it answered your call and your blood.

"The balance has been restored."

Somehow, it seemed as though things had ended a little too neatly. After the three days I'd had, I was more than a little skeptical.

"Alecca is gone?" I asked. "Isn't that going to screw up the whole three Fates thing?" I mean, even when the evil,

ominous fairy of doom had been playing hide-and-seek in the ocean, there had still been three Fates. And now that she was gone . . .

The woman looked at me and lifted a hand to caress the side of my face, breaking me from my thoughts. "All things said and done, the balance has a way of taking care of itself," she said. "Now that Alecca's hatred is gone from this world, things will right themselves. You will see."

"Okay. Death gone," I said. "That can't be too bad, right?"

The woman laughed. "Foolish child," she said affectionately. "Have you not eyes to see? Your Alecca was not who you assumed her to be."

"No?"

"No. Of Sister Life and Sister Death, she was the former. You mortals always think that Death is the enemy. Who better than the spinner of life would know how to spin your intimate desires into a deadly web? Who better than Life would understand you? Who other than Life could have known you as she did?"

We'd assumed Death was the evil one for obvious reasons . . . death equals bad, right? And yet, Alecca had matched my pyrokinesis and she'd messed with my mind, had made me see things that weren't there. Annabelle had been right. Sister Life did have the psychic and pyrokinetic powers. We just hadn't figured on fighting Life.

"No one ever does," the woman said. "Enough questions,

247

Bailey. It's time for you to return to your world, and I shall return to my sea."

I looked at the ocean beneath me and ran my hands along its surface. "Who are you?" I asked, unable to help myself.

"I am Sidhe," the woman said. "One of the first. I have been known by many names. Poseidon. Neptune. Triton. Among my kind, I am called Morgan."

And with that, she was gone.

I opened my eyes and found myself smack in the middle of our school gymnasium. I glanced around, half-expecting the others to be looking down at me, worried expressions on their faces, but as I sat up, I realized they were doing the same.

"Wow," Delia said. "Alecca . . . just wow. That was pretty unreal."

I snorted. If she thought that was unreal, wait until she heard about the little chat I'd just had with yet another Greek god/fairy hybrid.

It took me a full fifteen minutes to tell them the story.

"So Adea and Valgius are like your great-great-bazillion-times-great-grandparents?" Delia asked. "Freaky."

"Sweet," Zo said simply. "Does that mean you get to keep some of your powers?"

I opened my mouth and then closed it again. Did I?

"Speaking of powers," Delia said, "according to that clock, we only have our powers for like four more hours,

248

and Zo, so help me Gucci, you're going to scry for some hot guys before you lose your divination for good."

Zo groaned, and Annabelle and I broke into giggles.

"Come on," I told Zo. "Dance tonight. You could have a hot date." That reminded me . . . "Hey, Delia, who are you going to the dance with?"

"Thepizzaboy," Delia said in a rush.

"What?" I asked. "I couldn't understand you."

"The pizza boy," Delia said, tucking a strand of hair behind her ear. "You know, the guy who delivered our pizza."

"And he asked you when?" I waited patiently for Delia's answer.

"Last night," Delia said innocently. "I ordered pizza when I got home, and happened to mention that there was a dance tonight, and he just couldn't help himself. *Voilà!* Date."

Zo slung her arm around Delia's shoulder. "Tell me," she said seriously, "did he ask you or your breasts?"

Delia stuck her tongue out at Zo. "He asked all three of us, thank you very much."

Zo joined our giggling, and a moment later we were rolling around on the gym floor, laughing so hard we could barely breathe. It wasn't that funny, but I figured we could chalk it up to exhaustion. After what we'd been through, we deserved a laugh.

"Ahem."

At the sound of the voice, we broke off our giggling as best we could and turned toward the door.

The principal glared down at us. "Shouldn't you ladies be in class?" he asked.

"No," Zo said flatly. She elbowed Annabelle. "Tell him, A-belle."

Annabelle sat up and went into proper-miss mode. "You want us to take the rest of the day off," Annabelle told him. "We did a lovely job here."

Without warning, the principal began surveying the gym. "You girls did a lovely job here. You should take the rest of the day off."

"Them?" an outraged voice squealed from the doorway. "They didn't decorate the gym. They aren't even on the dance committee." Alexandra glared at us. "They don't belong here," she complained to the principal.

"Don't be ridiculous," the principal told her. "These girls did a fine job, and they're taking the rest of the day off, and you, Ms. Atkins, should be in class."

Alex's jaw dropped. "But . . . but . . ."

The four of us hooked arms and walked past her without saying a single word.

"You know," Delia said finally, "I'm going to miss these powers."

Chapter 21

"Yes, yes, sort of, and I am a genius." Delia pronounced her judgments on our outfits one by one as we stepped out of the car.

She and I were still the yeses. Annabelle, her long hair pulled out of her face except for a single wispy tendril, was the sort of. Delia was still holding a teeny tiny fashion grudge that A-belle wasn't wearing an outfit that Delia had picked out. As for Zo . . .

"This is the last time I'm ever wearing a dress." Zo grimaced as she made an attempt at walking, but her eyes were smiling. "Ever."

When Delia had turned Zo's T-shirt and jeans into the gorgeous black dress she'd tried on in Escape, I'd thought Zo was going to kill her, but after our brush with death (er . . . our brush with Life if you wanted to get technical), Zo had slung her arm around Delia's shoulder and told her to do her worst.

Delia Cameron wasn't the type of person who had to be asked twice.

So there we were, alive, gorgeous (well, in my case, passable), and walking through the gym door to the first official dance of the year.

"Ready?" Delia asked me, a huge grin on her face.

I took in the dance floor. "Ready for what?"

Ready for the deathfest this dance would have become if we hadn't stopped Alecca?

Ready for the scene I'd seen too many times before: the lights, the music, the shining decorations? I'd been seduced by it. I'd been so wrapped up in wanting it to be real, wanting Kane to like me back, that I'd almost sentenced this dance (and maybe the world) to complete and utter destruction.

There was no way I was ready for this.

"Confidence, Bay," Delia told me. "He *asked* you to save him a dance, remember?"

"Whatever." I wrapped my arms around my waist.

"No whatever," Delia said firmly. "You're here, you're gorgeous, your tattoo is showing just the right amount, and that outfit is to die for." Delia paused. "Annabelle, do your mind mojo. Tell her she's irresistible," she commanded.

A-belle bit back a grin. "Weeeeellllllll," she said teasingly. Zo jabbed her in the side.

"You look great, Bay," Annabelle said.

"There," Delia said, pointing. I groaned. Could she be any more conspicuous? "There he is. Go ask him to dance." She paused, waiting for me to obey, and when I didn't, she spoke again. "Now, Bay, before Alex superglues herself to his chest for the night."

I tried to rid myself of that mental image, but it was impossible, and I couldn't help but think that if it wasn't for us, Alex wouldn't have been able to superglue herself to anyone's chest ever again. Not that I expected a thank-you (which, by the way, would have been nice).

"You should ask him," Annabelle said quietly. "Ask him to dance." Almost immediately, I felt strangely compelled to ask Kane to dance.

"When do these powers wear off?" I asked, exasperated when I realized what Annabelle was doing.

Annabelle looked down at her watch. "Any time now," she said softly. "Just go."

"But what if there's some side effect and you guys need me and . . ." Frantically, I stalled.

"Bailey," Zo said, her hands on her hips. "Don't make me hurt you. Just go."

"But what if I set him on fire?" I asked. "If our powers aren't gone, and something makes me angry or upset or . . ."

"Bailey!" All three of them yelled my name at once, and whenever they team up on me like that, I have absolutely no choice. I bit my bottom lip, and with one last pathetic look at each of them, I turned around, mentally prepping myself to cross the dance floor to Kane.

Of course, since I was Bailey, queen of clumsiness, when I turned around I ran smack into a large, male-shaped object.

A Kane-shaped object.

"Hayl—" He stopped and corrected himself. "Bailey, right?"

"Yeah," I said, stumbling over the word.

Great, I thought. After all that—psychotic fairies, killer fantasies, magical powers—I *still* couldn't form a decipherable word around Mr. Eye Candy.

"You wanna dance?"

I opened my mouth and then closed it again.

"Yes," Delia hissed in my ear. Then she looked up at Kane. "She'd love to," she said smoothly, "and," she added, eyeing her own date, "so would I."

The pizza boy (whose name none of us, including Delia, knew) took the hint, and led Delia (and her breasts) onto the dance floor.

As she passed me, I saw a flash of blue-green light.

Sidhe blue. Blood green.

I turned around and looked down just in time to see Zo's tattoo darken to black and in the next instant fade from her foot entirely. Annabelle's hand went to the back of her neck, and even without checking, I knew that her tattoo was gone as well.

It was over. No more tattoos. No more powers. Things were back to normal.

"Uhhh . . . Bailey?"

Except, of course, for the fact that the hottest guy in school was actually talking to me. That was extremely un-normal.

"Right," I said out loud, mentally berating myself for it even as I said it. "Kane." I'd almost forgotten about him.

"So you know my name," he said, "and I know your name." He paused. "So now can we dance?"

Completely unable to speak, I nodded.

I put my hands on his shoulders, and he put his loosely around my waist. We swayed, completely out of rhythm with the music. He stepped on my foot four times.

It was great.

As we moved awkwardly back and forth, my hands decided to start sweating, but even that couldn't remove the dopey grin from my face.

Kane struggled to make conversation. "Your hair," he said finally.

Your hair looks like moonlight.

"It's . . . uhhhh . . . nice."

My cheeks warmed. He thought my hair was nice. It wasn't moonlight, he wasn't in love with me, and I was a horrible dancer. This wasn't my fantasy. It was real.

The second the song ended, he dropped his hands from my waist. "Thanks," he said.

"You're wel—" I was in the process of accepting his thanks and simultaneously shifting my weight from one foot to the other when my ankle rolled beneath me, and I went toppling onto the floor. From the corner of my eye, I saw Marissa Baker, newspaper goody-goody, snap a photo of my fall, with my luck, for a front-page story: GIRL LOSES FOOTING OVER HOTTIE.

The hottie in question reached down to help me up, and I could feel my body warming with a blush. It spread from my cheeks down my neck and to the small of my back.

Absolutely mortified, I pulled my top down and tried to appear cool, calm, and collected.

"You know, you're pretty cute when you do that," Kane said.

My mouth dropped open and the heat drained from my body. Cute? He thought I was cute? Cute when I did what? Blush? Fall? I made a mental note to blush and fall more often.

"And that tattoo is awesome," Kane added. "Is it real?"

"Tattoo?" I repeated dumbly. My heart started beating faster and I could feel the blood rushing through my veins. "What tattoo?"

Twisting my body, I turned. There, in the middle of my back, like a sun rising out of my skirt, was a tattoo the color of Sídhe blood.

It's in the blood. Things of power always are.

My power. My tattoo.

You are Sídhe, Bailey. Adea and Valgius spoke in my

mind, and it took me a moment to process the fact that they were all right. *And you are ours.*

"Is it real?"

For a second, I thought Kane was asking about the voice in my head, but then I realized that (duh) he was referring to the tattoo. I brushed my fingers lightly over it, and it flashed once, brilliantly, in my mind.

Always. You are Sidhe. Always.

"Yeah," I said after a moment. "It's real."

I scanned the dance floor for my friends, and when the music ended, I did what I needed to do. "Listen," I said, and I couldn't believe I was saying it. "I have to go."

Kane looked at me and then nodded. "Okay," he said, "but maybe we could, you know, dance later?"

It wasn't telling me that he knew me and wanted me and loved me, but it was a start. I nodded and worked my way over to Annabelle and Zo.

"How was it?" they asked in unison.

"Yeah . . . was it great or was it great?" Delia asked, joining us. "I sent pizza boy to get some punch so we could talk, so dish. Why aren't you still over there? Did you kiss? Did he say anything about your shoes? I really love those shoes. . . ."

"It was . . ." How was I supposed to describe my dance with Kane? It hadn't really been magical. At all.

But it had been real, I reminded myself, and remembering the actual feeling of him stepping on my feet and

257

telling me I was cute, I smiled. "It was nice," I finished. "And you'll never guess what else."

"What?" all three of them asked immediately.

I turned around and lifted my top up just a little. "Check out my tattoo."

Zo's mouth dropped open. "It's still there," she said.

"And perfectly positioned, if I do say so myself," Delia added, overcoming her surprise more quickly than the others.

"Bailey," Annabelle said softly. "That's not your tattoo."

"What?" I twisted around, trying to get a better look at it.

"You know, you're right, A-belle," Delia said. "It's a little more complicated than Bailey's old one. Sophisticated. Chic."

Managing to contort myself enough to get a better look at the tattoo, I saw immediately what they were talking about. It looked like my tattoo at first glance, a sun symbol that I knew by now meant fire, but there was another layer to it, another design interwoven with my own.

"It's like mine," Annabelle said. She lifted her hand and carefully traced the crescent shapes with her finger.

Everyone else had lost their tattoos, and somehow, I'd ended up with mine *and* Annabelle's?

It's the symbol for life.

It took me a moment to realize that Annabelle hadn't made the observation out loud.

Knowledge and fire. Annabelle's tattoo and mine, and now, I was hearing Annabelle's thoughts.

"Alecca is gone? Isn't that going to screw up the three Fates thing?"

"All things said and done, the balance has a way of taking care of itself. . . ."

My exchange with the woman who had called herself Morgan rang in my head.

"Now that Alecca's hatred is gone from this world, things will right themselves. You will see."

"Do you still have your . . . you know . . . ?" Annabelle asked, making wiggly motions with her fingers.

"More importantly," Zo said, her brow wrinkled in thought, "do you have Annabelle's?"

At that exact moment, I intercepted what Zo would have almost definitely defined as an incriminating thought.

"Uhhh . . . maybe."

Zo groaned.

"And there's . . . ummm . . . a slight chance that I may be . . ." I mumbled the end of the sentence.

"Fur feet?" Delia asked, straining to hear.

"No," Annabelle said, an awed smile creeping onto her face. "The third Fate." Her mind started working out the logic of the whole thing, and mine swam with her mental words. "Alecca's gone, and her powers went into Bailey. That's why she still has the tattoo—it's the mark of Life."

259

Well, if anyone's going to be in my head, Zo told me silently, *at least it's you.*

"Okay, so Bailey's the third Fate," Delia said, taking things in stride. "Coolness."

I'd started out this whole adventure with three best friends who all knew their place in this world a little better than I did, and I'd ended up with a destiny that I couldn't quite wrap my mind around, but when it came right down to it, the important thing had stayed exactly the same.

Delia linked her arm through mine. "Well, Ms. Fate," she said, "if I still had my power, I'd transmogrify us something to toast with."

Zo shrugged and, moving surprisingly well to the beat of the music, she raised her fist. "To Bailey's tattoo," she said. "May her mother never find out about it."

"To stopping Alecca," Annabelle added.

"To us," Delia said. "For being so fabulous."

I bit back a smile, and the four of us air-toasted as we danced. Some things never changed.

ACKNOWLEDGMENTS

As always, I owe a great debt to the people who sweated over this book with the same passion I did. Thanks to Elizabeth Harding, who helped me find Annabelle; Krista Marino, who had even bigger plans for Bailey than I did; and Marsha Barnes, who never stopped loving Delia and Zo. In writing a book about four friends, I was incredibly blessed to share the process with intelligent, insightful people whom I consider just that. Working with you all continues to be an absolute joy.

I also owe a great deal to the friends who saw me through writing, editing, and everything in between. This book spanned our last two years of college, and I couldn't have asked for better people to spend that time with. Thanks to Jackie Kim, for suddenly developing an insane love of young adult literature as a form of procrastination; to Neha Mahajan, for an always-open ear and an incredibly quick wit/smart mouth; to Ellie Marshall, who I'm convinced could probably single-handedly save the world from apocalypse; and to Amy Hart and Sarah Jones, for getting more excited than I was at every single development in this process. You guys are the best.

Many thanks also to the rest of the people whose support has meant more than I can say over the last two years: my family, Mom, Dad, Justin, and Allison; Laurie Santos—the best advisor a girl could ask for; and everyone at the Blue Board for being there from day one. I am extremely grateful to you all.

ABOUT THE AUTHOR

Jennifer Lynn Barnes is a recent graduate of Yale University, where she and her closest friends formed a society so secret she can't even tell you about it. She's not sure what her forte is, but when she's not writing, she enjoys researching animal and child cognition and shopping for sparkly accessories. Jennifer doesn't have a tattoo, but if she did, it would be small, blue green, and on her lower back. *Tattoo* is Jennifer Lynn Barnes's second novel. Her third, *Platinum*, the companion to *Golden*, will be out in the fall of 2007.